Street Pharm

Allison van Diepen

Simon Pulse
New York • London • Toronto • Sydney

SIMON PULSE
An imprint of Simon & Schuster Children's Publishing Division
1230 Avenue of the Americas, New York, NY 10020
Copyright © 2006 by Allison van Diepen
All rights reserved, including the right of reproduction in whole or in part in any form.
SIMON PULSE and colophon are registered trademarks of Simon & Schuster, Inc.
Designed by Steve Kennedy
The text of this book was set in Electra.
Manufactured in the United States of America
First Simon Pulse edition July 2006
10 9 8 7 6 5 4 3 2
Library of Congress Control Number 2005933468
ISBN-13: 978-1-4169-1154-8
ISBN-10: 1-4169-1154-5

FOR ELIZABETH VAN DIEPEN,

A.K.A. "G." THE COOLEST GRANDMA EVER.

My heartfelt thanks:

To Michelle Nagler at Simon Pulse for her unflagging
enthusiasm and faith in this book.

To my family for their love and support.

To my former students at Sheepshead Bay High School
in Brooklyn for a lifetime of inspiration.

And to Dan Hooker, my extraordinary agent, who
passed away several months after the sale of this
book. Thank you for helping me realize my dream.

TYRONE JOHNSON, SELF-MADE MAN

"WHAT ARE YOU GONNA BE WHEN YOU GROW UP?" THAT'S what most kids got asked.

Not me.

Mom always asked me what I *wasn't* gonna be, and you know what she wanted me to say?

A dealer, stealer, free-wheeler, player, hater, a downright dog—that's what my dad was.

When I came home from school, Mom was on the couch watching *Dr. Phil*. As usual.

"How was school, baby?"

"Good." No way I was gonna tell her I got kicked out. Really ass-to-the-curb kicked out this time. Starting tomorrow, I was supposed to show up at some alternative school.

"You working hard?"

"Yeah." Sweet, clueless Mom never noticed that I hadn't carried a book bag since the ninth grade.

"There's beef patties in the oven."

I checked the clock: 3:37 p.m. She'd be getting up from the sofa in about three minutes, getting ready for fifteen, and out the door in twenty.

When the commercial came on, Mom went to her room. I attacked the patties, only stopping to add more ketchup. A few minutes later, she came back into the kitchen in her grocery store uniform, her name tag already pinned on like she was proud or something. "You working tonight?" she asked me.

"Yeah." I gave up my cheek for a kiss while guzzling o.j., and she threw on her coat and hurried out the door.

Mom thought I worked at the Flatbush Sports Club on Atlantic Avenue. I ain't worked there a day in my life—but the manager owed me. He was one of my customers.

Time to get down to this brother's *real* bread-and-butter.

I took out my cell and speed-dialed Sonny.

"Ty! What the fuck's going on? Why'd you turn off your cell?"

"Mind your business. What's going on?"

"I need your help, son. Tonight we got us some deliveries."

"Already got some."

"Well, I got more for you."

"Go on."

I wrote the stuff in my Palm Pilot.

"Hold up," I said, "who's this Schultz guy?"

"A new customer I met last week. Told him we was getting a shipment with the hottest shit this side of Bogotá. He gonna drop five Gs!"

"You ain't kidding. How'd he find out about us?"

"In the fucking yellow pages."

"Seriously, Sonny, who told him?"

"Who? Shit, like he was gonna tell me! What, you think his friend wants a finder's fee or something?"

"Listen, if you so confident about him, *you* make the delivery."

"Can't, I promised Desarae we'd see a late movie. Schultz wants the stuff at ten."

"I'm not making this delivery unless you gimme some reason to think he ain't a cop."

"Ty, this guy ain't 5-o. Don't you think I can sniff out a cop by now?"

"I ain't risking my neck on your sense of smell, Sonny. Tell Michael Brown to make the delivery."

Michael Brown.

That little brother'd win the award for the most eager young hustler in Flatbush.

Quick, reliable.

Fourteen years old.

"A'ight, I'll tell Michael," Sonny said. "He can drop some stuff off at the Wilkes place, too."

That was what I liked about Sonny. He talked the shit, but when push came to shove, he always backed down. He knew the game was in my blood.

A SIMPLE BUSINESSMAN

BRRRRRINNNGGGG!!!

Cursing, I grabbed the phone beside my bed. "Yo."

"Is this Tyrone Johnson?" A white woman's voice.

"He ain't here. Who's this?"

"This is Ms. Bregman calling from the Les Chancellor Institute of Career Opportunities. Tyrone was expected here at nine o'clock this morning, but he hasn't arrived."

"He's at a meeting of the YDDA." *Young Drug Dealers of America. Ha-ha.*

"The what?"

"It's a co-op placement. You know. Sheepshead Bay High School arranged it. Hasn't your school been told that he ain't transferring no more?"

"Uh, no." Papers shuffling. "I was under the impression—"

"I know, ma'am, you just doing your job. But my younger brother is being watched over by an excellent team at Sheepshead, like Mr. Otto, the school psychologist and Mr. Edelstone, in Guidance. I think he's better off there. I worry about the sorta kids he'll meet at Les Chancellor."

"Oh, I didn't realize that was a concern. At any rate, I'll be in touch with Sheepshead to confirm that he's not transferring."

"I'm sure they sent you a fax about it yesterday. Finding that might save you some phone tag. Have a good day."

"You, too, Ty."

Click.

I blinked. Did she just say *Ty*? Or did she say, *You, too, bye?*

Ah, I was just being paranoid. Women always bought the shit I sold them. She was going to spend five minutes looking for the fax, not find it, and then call the house of the next kid who didn't show up, and not follow up on me until next month, if ever.

So much for all that *no child left behind* shit. I counted on being left behind, and left alone.

Seeing my cell blinking, I got out of bed, adjusted my balls, and reached for the phone.

Two messages.

Both from Sonny.

"Ty, have you seen Michael Brown? He was supposed to drop the money off an hour ago. This is making me real nervous. What the hell are you doing? You in bed or something?"

Next message. "Man, oh man, thank God you didn't make the delivery! You won't believe the shit that's gone down! Michael got locked up. You were so damn right about Schultz! I stopped by Michael's project to see if anybody'd peeped him, and they told me that the po-po was just there talking to his mom. Scary shit! Whatever, Michael ain't got no record, so he'll be in juvey a few months, it's no biggie. He won't talk. He knows our deal. Holla at you later."

I snapped the phone shut.

My instincts came through.

Too bad about Michael Brown.

Well, Michael knew what he was getting into. I'd warned him myself. Anyway, we gave our runners a good deal: If you do time and keep your trap shut, we'll pay you ten Gs when you get out. It was fair. And my conscience was clear.

I took a shower, then put on an *Ultimate Fighting* tape

as I was eating breakfast. I loved this shit. Ultimate Fighting was real, unlike most of the garbage on TV, and man, was it bloody. Royce Gracie was one of the best fighters, and it wasn't because he was a big guy. No, he just had the right moves.

I got my height (all six feet two inches) from my dad, and I was getting more muscular every day. I took Creatine and ate protein bars all the time. Of course, you gotta work out, too. I go to the gym at least five times a week.

I looked at my genuine Rolex. I put it on every day after my shower, before I even put on my clothes. It reminded me that time is money.

Time management is everything. If a brother wanna get ahead, he gotta use every minute to better himself. Everything I did made me better—tougher, stronger, richer, smarter—or I didn't do it.

Take high school. A waste of time. Nobody there taught me what I needed to survive on the streets.

I learned all the math I needed by the seventh grade, and a calculator helped me with the rest.

History class didn't teach me nothing I couldn't learn by watching movies like *Glory* or *Malcolm X*.

Gym class didn't show me sports skills I couldn't learn on the court or on TV.

My point? By the time I was fourteen, I knew school wasn't gonna be nothing but a place of business.

NETWORKING

SHEEPSHEAD BAY HIGH.

Population: thirty-eight hundred students, two hundred staff, and eleven security guards.

Location: Avenue X, between Bedford and Batchelder. Big as Yankee Stadium, the school takes up a whole city block.

As I walked through the metal detectors, one of the guards stopped me. "What you doing here, Johnson? Heard you got transferred."

"Yeah. I gotta clear out my locker."

He waved me in.

I got there just before the bell rang to end sixth period. I went to a back stairway going from the basement to the gym. Lots of kids passed me, some actually trying not to be late for their next class. When I saw my employee, I grabbed her arm. "How you doing, Clarissa?"

"Hey!" She gave me a hug, squashing her big titties against my chest. The chick was dripping with perfume. "What's popping, Ty?"

"Me, if you keep doing that." I looked her up and down with a grin. She loved that. Clarissa Sanchez been trying to get with me for years.

With those pouty lips and that diamond stud in her nose, she was a hottie. But hooking up with an employee was too risky. Piss her off, and next thing you know she was snitching to the po-po.

"Did you hear about Michael Brown getting locked up for making a delivery to an undercover cop?" she said, like she was the shit because she knew what the whole neighborhood knew by now.

"What you say his name was?"

"Michael Brown."

"Should I know him?"

"No, he just a kid, no one even knew he was dealing. Serves him right for tryna be big-time."

Clarissa had no idea that Michael Brown was on my payroll. Hell, she didn't even know that I had a partner

named Sonny or that I had another hustler in this
school.

"Listen, Clarissa, you got enough stuff to last the week?"

"Yeah, but I'm working on a couple new customers. If I
need more, I'll let you know."

"I'll find you next Friday night at The Cellar for the cash."

"Right. I'll be there with my new man. He's twenty-five."

"Stop, you making me jealous." I patted her ass. "Get to
class, sexy lady."

"See ya, Ty."

I watched her swing her ass as she went upstairs. I walked
away, shaking my head.

I found my next contact ten minutes later on the basketball
court. I took off my shirt and joined the game, working up a
good sweat. The hoops lost their nets years ago, but it didn't
matter. I liked the solid sound of the ball bouncing off the
backboard and dropping through the basket without the
catch of the net.

Rob Monfrey had a mouth full of metal and bad personal hygiene. His hair was so nappy, I didn't even wanna
think about what was lost in there. But he was a good
employee because he stuck his snotty nose in everybody's

business. He knew who was doing what, where, when, and who their mother was screwing. No one kept their mouth shut around him because no one took him serious.

Big mistake.

Monfrey hustled rock *and* information. He was more important to my business than Clarissa could ever be.

For helping me out, I kept his cash flow going and his weed habit satisfied. He'd cut off his right arm before he'd lose this sweet deal.

"Didn't think I'd be seeing you here, Ty," Monfrey said while he was trying to cover me. "Thought you was kicked out."

Another thing about Monfrey: He spent most of his days hanging around the guidance offices, keeping his ears open.

"I *was*."

"What you do this time?"

"Nothing. Edelstone thought that was a problem." I caught a pass, dribbled twice, and sank a jump shot.

"Nice shot!" one of the guys said.

"Wow!" Monfrey clapped his hands, looking like a jackass.

After the game, Monfrey and me talked business, then I headed for the bus stop.

I had enough money to buy me a shiny, fast ride, but I took the bus. Why?

Because I was smart. Because buying those things would give the cops an invitation to go digging. They knew I was Orlando's son, and they'd be fools not to suspect I was dealing. The second I slipped up, the second I got cocky, they'd be right there waiting. My dad's biggest weakness was the way he flashed his money. I wasn't going to make the same mistake. Eventually I'd open a legit business that would give me a cover for all my green.

In the meantime, I practiced one of man's most important skills.

Patience.

A SHORT PIECE ON PACKING

I DIDN'T OWN NO GUN.

Having a gun wasn't gonna change my chances of getting shot. You don't hear about people saving themselves from drive-bys by shooting back. If you shoot back and you lucky enough to survive the drive-by, you still got the cops charging your ass.

Worse, you killed a bystander.

The best way not to get hit was to have homies. I got Blood homies and Crip homies, brothers who respected my business and knew I didn't take sides. Brothers who heard of my father when they were little. Brothers who knew the Johnsons were an institution.

That ain't to say they hadn't tested me. But I never faced a test that me and my two fists couldn't handle.

SURPRISES

I CAME HOME AROUND MIDNIGHT TO SOMETHING I HATED.

A surprise.

I found her sitting in the kitchen, drumming her fake nails on the table. She was still in her work uniform and had a glass of soda in front of her.

I recognized the look on her face.

The look of mean.

"Where the hell were you today?"

"School. Then work."

"*Ha!*" She slammed her fist on the table. "I ain't buying this shit from you! I know you wasn't at school today. Maybe I should call that manager of yours to see if you was really at work, too! How am I to know you ain't running the streets like your good-for-nothing daddy?"

"Mom, you tripping."

"*Sit* down, Ty. Don't stand over me like you the big man. Sit down."

I got comfortable, knowing this would take a while.

"Your guidance counselor called today. He said you been kicked out of Sheepshead and you were supposed to start this morning at one of those"— she twisted her lips —"*alternative* schools. Not only did you not tell me any of this, you didn't even show up! They say you tried to convince the secretary that you was an older brother and there was no transfer!"

I stared at the floor. With Mom, I had to play it cool. "I messed up. I'm sorry."

"Sorry don't pay the rent, damn it!" She leaned so far over the table that our foreheads almost touched. "You gonna finish high school whether you like it or not. After that, do whatever the hell you want. Don't forget, you under my authority till you turn eighteen."

That was less than seven months away. Fact was, I hadn't been under her authority since I was a kid. Sure, she asked questions like any other mom. But I was such a good liar that she usually believed my answers.

"They expecting you Monday at nine. Be there, or you can pack your bags."

"I will, Mom." I meant it. Living at home was a damn good cover for my business. And who knows? This new school could be a chance to get new customers.

Mom stared at me, hard. "You walk that line, baby boy. I know you don't like school, but you promised me you'd stick it out. I don't wanna be doubting my own son. But Ty, if I find out you be dealing or gangbanging . . ."

"Chill, Mom, chill. You know it ain't like that. Monday, call the school to see if I showed up." I put my hand over hers and gave her my best smile. "Pack me peanut butter and jelly, yo?"

She gave a sad smile. "All right."

LUNCHING IT UP

NEXT DAY. SONNY'S FLY RIDE—A 1980 CADILLAC WITH pimped-out rims—swung into the parking lot, where I waited for him. Sonny never came within a mile of my crib. If Mom ever saw us together, she'd know what's up. She knew Sonny from his days as my dad's right-hand man.

I could tell by the loose turn that he was on his damn phone. He braked just inches from my shoes. The tinted window came down. "What's cracking?" He grinned, gold teeth flashing. "Gimme a sec. Old lady's got PMS." Into the phone he said, "Nah, baby, I didn't mean it like that. I ain't making no fun. . . ."

I got in, slapping him five. I leaned back against the leather seat as Sonny drove out of the parking lot and headed for the city.

Sonny Blake was twenty-eight years old. When my dad got locked up, he gave control to Sonny until I was ready to take charge. That time came sooner than they expected. By the time I was sixteen, I was a pro.

Sonny saw himself as a bad boy. He had the clothes, the ride, the bling. Problem was, he was all mush when it came to the women in his life—he totally spoiled his mama and sister, and he was crazy devoted to his girlfriend Desarae.

Sonny didn't get off the phone until we walked into the restaurant. La Tranquilla was one of the swankiest Italian places in Lower Manhattan. Two homies strolling in always made jaws drop. That's why Sonny loved going there in the first place. He got off on being noticed.

"Good afternoon, gentlemen." The hostess, a slim white girl with shiny black hair, led us to a choice table.

"Excellent table, Jeanine." Sonny winked at her as he sat down.

"I'm pleased you like it, Mr. Blake." She smiled and walked away.

Sonny glanced around. "I know what they thinking."

"The only brothers who can afford to eat here must be hustlers."

He laughed. Loud. "They be fucking right!"

I scanned the menu for something with chicken and then snapped it shut. Sonny spent a good five minutes looking, but in the end he went for filet mignon, as usual.

After we gave our order, I said, "Let's talk Schultz. We both know it ain't Michael Brown they want, it's the guys at the top."

"The guys at the top are in fucking Colombia! But I know what you saying. Met Schultz at Woody's Pub. He put the word out that he wanted to cop some rocks, so I went up to him. He didn't know who I was."

"Good." I took a sip of water. "Why'd you tell me you got his name from another customer?"

"I never said that. . . . You assumed it." He hiked his chin. "Know what happens when you assume?"

You make an ass outta you and me. Fucking comedian, Sonny.

"Why'd you let me assume it, then?"

"I thought he was legit."

My hand tightened around my glass. "Yeah, well, I'm glad you didn't convince me."

Sonny nodded. "Me too."

"You watch your back, Sonny. Schultz knows your face now. Po-po's looking for you."

"The fuck I care. I bet he wouldn't even be able to pick me out of a lineup. To white guys, all black guys look the same. I ain't scared."

"I ain't saying be scared. Just be careful. They wanna know who Michael Brown's really working for."

Sonny grunted. "They gonna grill that boy bad. Don't matter. Michael know it don't pay to be a snitch."

"Fo sho."

The waiter returned with a basket of bread. Glad to forget about Michael Brown, we dug in.

KNOW THY ENEMY

ENEMIES ARE A GIFT, NOT A CURSE. ENEMIES FORCE A BROTHER to be on top of his game.

Back in junior high, I swiped a copy of *The Art of War* from the public library. My Tae Kwon Do instructor used to quote it all the time. It was written hundreds of years ago by some Chinese guy named Sun Tzu, but I felt like it was written just for me.

I used some of what I learned in that book to make up my own personal code.

1. Know your enemies. Understand them. Figure out their next move before they do.
2. Never show weakness.
3. Rely on number one, no one else.

4. Control your physical instincts. Don't let anybody pressure you
   into sex or into a fight unless you're in control of the situation.

I lived by those rules every day of my life.

Sunday I met an enemy I didn't know I had.

Like most other Sundays, I went to the mall, my homeboy
Cheddar by my side. He was one of my oldest friends. We
been hanging since he moved to Brooklyn from Atlanta in
the fourth grade.

Cheddar—I gave him that nickname because he used to
get off on cutting the cheese in class—was the anchor of the
Sheepshead Bay High School track team. His life was all
about sports, and I gave him props for that.

It was good to have homies outside the business. I wanted
to keep it that way. So when Cheddar asked questions about
my dealing, I didn't say much. Eventually he stopped asking.

The mall was crowded with shoppers. Cheddar and me
smiled at the girls. We gave real big smiles to the girls carrying those sassy pink and white Victoria's Secret bags. We
knew *exactly* what they were trying to say.

I bought Sean John gear and a pair of kicks. Total price
tag: $634.

On our way out of a sports store, a girl stepped in my way.

"*Ty Johnson.* You ain't easy to track down."

"Do I know you?" I didn't recognize her, and she had a face you wouldn't forget. She had a too-wide nose, too-thick eyebrows and a tight little mouth. Maybe it was the expression on her face that made her so ugly.

"You don't know who I am, Ty Johnson. But I know *you.* I know all about *you!*"

This was gonna be bad. Time to bounce. I turned to walk away. Then I felt my jersey yanked so hard, it cut into my Adam's apple.

"Don't you dare walk away from me. You wanna know who I am? I'm Shanequa Brown. Michael's sister."

"Shanequa who?"

"You got a helluva lot of nerve playing dumb to my face. My brother went down for you, *bitch.*"

If she was a guy, she'd be tasting my fist. But she knew I wasn't gonna hit no girl, especially with a whole lot of people watching.

"I think you got it wrong, honey."

I knew the slap was coming, but I didn't try to block it. "You think you *all dat*, but you just a fool. *I* ain't afraid of

you, Ty Johnson. And I'll enjoy watching you go down." She
spit on my shoe and walked away.

Everyone stared at me. I could feel their eyes burning all
over my body like cigarettes. Fuck them. Fuck *her*.

Cheddar said, "Yo, let's go grab some eats."

THE REAL WORLD

EVEN WHEN I WAS A KID, DAD DIDN'T HIDE THE UGLY SIDE OF the business from me.

Once, when I was nine, I went with him to a run-down apartment building in East Flatbush. It was a cold night in January, and I tried to keep my Jordans out of the slush as I got out of the car and followed him up the sidewalk.

"This gonna take long?" I asked in the elevator. "I'm hungry."

"This'll be quick."

We got off on the third floor, turning down a gloomy hall-way. "Remember, watch where you step in there," Dad said. "There could be needles or cat crap on the floor." He knocked on the door.

It swung open. A stick-thin white lady with messy brown

hair leaned against the door jamb. "It's about time, Orlando. Get in here."

I looked around. The place was disgusting. Pizza boxes and take-out food wrappers were scattered over the floor. The litter box, right beside the door, overflowed with cat shit. Two cats, so skinny it looked like they hadn't eaten in weeks, eyed me like I was dinner.

The woman pulled a wad of cash from her pocketbook and stuffed it into my dad's hand. He uncrumpled the bills and counted them. "Hundred short, honey."

She ran a bony hand through her hair. "Don't have it. I barely got customers anymore. It's too damn cold. No one's out."

Dad made a *tsk-tsk* sound. "Ain't my problem."

Movement caught my eye. A little kid waddled out of the bedroom. I watched as the kid climbed onto the torn-up sofa.

"Dad." I tapped his shoulder and pointed to the kid.

He shrugged off my hand.

"But, Dad—"

"*Quiet.*" He handed the lady her rock. "If you don't have the difference for me next week, I'm cutting you off. Got me?"

She nodded.

We walked out.

I kept quiet all the way back to the car.

Dad started the engine and turned to me. "You done?"

"What?"

"Sucking your teeth."

"But didn't you see she had a kid in there? It's just, she a ho, ain't she?"

"None of that be our business." He pulled onto the road. "Tell me, what do you think would happen if I stopped supplying her? You think she'd go to rehab?"

"I guess she'd get it from somebody else."

"Right, she'd find any old hustla and throw cash at him. You know what would happen then? He'd see her for the cheap crack whore she is, and give her his worst cut. She'd O.D., and the neighbors would find her cat-eaten body after a week, when the smell got so bad, they couldn't take it no more."

"Ughh."

"That lady, she made herself a junkie—I didn't have nothing to do with it. All I do is supply her with good quality shit. The minute she decides to clean up, I'll tell her, *Good for you, I'm prouda you.*"

"But then she won't be your customer no more."

"I got plenty of customers. The little ones like her don't add up to much at the end of the week. She used to bring in other customers for me, but she don't no more. I'd be happy if she got control of her life." He braked at a stop light and looked at me. "The worst thing a man can do in his life is to lose control. Take the first time I did crack. I wasn't much older than you. Best fucking feeling I ever had, but it was too good to keep under control. So I never did it again. You get what I'm saying?"

I nodded. Never lose control.

"Ty, when people do drugs, they ain't nothing but slaves—not to their dealers, but to the drugs. And most of the hos out there, they be slaves to the drugs *and* their pimps."

"That's wack."

"Yeah, but that's democracy. People make they own choices, even if they be stupid ones. Look at your uncle Jean. My own brother, and I can't do nothing to stop him from killing himself. We can't let these things get us down, Ty. Look at us. We rich, the ladies love us." He patted my head. "Let's get us some pizza."

WELCOME TO THE LES CHANCELLOR INSTITUTE OF CAREER OPPORTUNITIES

LES CHANCELLOR WAS IN A CHEWED-UP (AND SPIT-OUT) East New York hood. The grass in front of the school was fenced off, I guess because they didn't trust people not to mess it up.

When I went inside and saw the metal detectors and security guards, I knew I was at one of two places: a high school or a prison.

One security guard went through my bag. Another frisked me.

"Yo, ain't walking through metal detectors enough?"

The guard glared at me. "You new. Let me tell you this. We doing you a favor. Get it?"

"Got it."

"Good. Now if you here for nine o'clock orientation, you five minutes late."

"At Sheepshead, we call that mad early."

"This ain't no regular school, son."

"Well, maybe I'm at the wrong place."

"Doubt it."

I could get used to this place, I thought an hour later as I walked into the classroom and zeroed in on a couple of shorties. I made eye contact with the one in the tight skirt. She smiled back, uncrossing her legs and crossing them again, giving me a peep of her panties.

Total nympho.

Another cute girl rolled her eyes and gave me a look that said, *You interrupted our class. Wipe that smile off your face and sit your ass down.*

I liked her already.

The dean left me at the door. The teacher (fortyish-bald-eagle) put down his chalk. "Tyrone Johnson, is it?"

"Ty."

"Welcome, Ty. I'm Mr. Guzman. We've been expecting you. A few days behind schedule, but you've found your way, and that's what matters. Why don't you take a seat behind Darius?" He pointed to a seat, third from the front, behind a guy in a Lakers jersey.

Was he playing? Third from the front! No thank you.

He saw the look on my face. "Sit there for now. If you find it uncomfortable after a few days, we'll work out a better arrangement."

We were gonna work out a better arrangement *after class.* I walked to my seat, checking out the posters of historical people on the walls. Famous quotes had been put up too. One was from Gandhi: "Nonviolence is the greatest force at the disposal of mankind."

Yeah, right. Put Gandhi in Brooklyn for a day.

I sat down and pulled a notebook out of my bag.

Too bad I forgot a damn pen.

Shit. Wasn't like me to forget nothing. But then, I hadn't brought a pen to school in years.

"Psst." The nympho twirled a pen between her fingers and passed it to me.

"Thanks."

"Kristina." She gave me a great big smile.

"Beautiful name."

Mr. Guzman looked at me. "All set, Ty?"

"Yeah."

"Good. We were just reviewing the causes of World War One. Jamal?"

"That guy got shot."

"Do you remember his name?"

"Uh . . . Archie something."

"You mean Archduke Ferdinand." Mr. Guzman wrote the name on the board. "Yes, his assassination was the immediate cause that sparked the war. What about long-term causes? Alyse?"

So that's what her name was. Alyse, that too-serious shorty, said, "Alliances between countries. And economic rivalries—each country wanted to have more colonies than the others."

"Excellent." He wrote *alliances* and *economic rivalries* on the board. "What's another one?"

"Lots of big-ass weapons," a guy at the back called out.

"Yes, militarism. That's when everyone wants to build up their armies and weaponry because they know their rivals are doing the same. What's another reason?"

Mr. Guzman waited and waited. Finally Alyse put her hand up again. "Propaganda."

"Right. The press was full of war talk before anything ever happened. The media played a major role in raising tensions."

"As usual," I grumbled.

"Pardon, Ty?"

I said, "Well, that's what TV and newspapers do—cause trouble. They always talking trash to make money."

"There's certainly some validity to that."

"'Course there is. The news is what started that whole East Coast–West Coast thing."

"Hmm. Could you clarify that for us? I'm afraid I don't know much about this East Coast–West Coast conflict."

"You heard about Tupac Shakur and Notorious B.I.G. being knocked off, right? Well, they was rappers from each coast, and they got offed 'cause they was at war."

"What started this war?"

"Same kinda thing that you be talking about. They was competing to sell records, peeps was taking sides, guys on each side was strapped and hiring gangstas to back them up."

"That's a fascinating connection to make. So, class, if Ty is able to make such a strong comparison, what does all this tell us about the causes of war?"

"They all the same," Nympho said.

"Not necessarily," Alyse said. "There's one other thing we haven't talked about, because it doesn't apply to World War

One, but it does apply to World War Two and a few wars since. A dictator. Someone like Hitler or Stalin. Or that Serbian guy with the weird name."

"Slobodan Milošević?" Mr. Guzman said. "You've made a good point. So we can see that wars stem from a variety of causes, from rivalries to ambitious dictators. Will there always be war, do you think?"

A guy in Blood colors shot his hand up. "War's what humans do. Man is a savage beast."

A Latina said, "That's a man's excuse. War only happens because *men* are too stupid to find another way."

"We can't generalize like that," Alyse said. "World War One, yeah, I think it didn't have to happen. But not all wars are like that. Someone like Hitler had to be stopped with violence. He wasn't going to quit until he'd taken over the whole world and killed every Jew and other minority in it."

Mr. Guzman scratched his cheek. "Now here's a question. Should a country start a war because they *think* another country will come after them in the future?"

"Like what happened in Iraq?" someone asked.

"I'm saying in general."

I put my hand up. I *had* to answer this one.

"Ty?"

"A good leader always knows his enemy's next move, and strikes first. Think about it. Who got it made? The army that gets to the battlefield first, or second?"

Mr. Guzman's eyes brightened. *"The Art of War."*

I nodded.

Alyse said, "That *sounds* fine, but is it really smart to go around starting wars just *in case* you think an enemy might strike against you? Like when Bush went after Saddam Hussein. Now he's got even more of the Arab world against him. Against us. Is it worth it to get rid of one enemy if you're going to make lots more? I don't think so."

The Blood said, "Saddam needed to be taken out. We knew what we had to do, and we did it. That's why we on top and why we staying there."

Alyse shook her head. "That's why America has so many enemies, because we have to be on top! What about changing our reputation so that we're seen as a peaceful, caring country?"

"Never gonna happen," I said.

Before she could say anything, the bell rang.

As I was packing up my books, I could tell Alyse was watching me. But when I looked up, she turned away.

I timed it so that we got to the door at the same time. Letting her go ahead of me, I said, "Sounds like you know your stuff, honey."

"Thanks. And do me a favor?"

"Yeah?"

"Don't call me honey."

I went to all my classes that day. I ain't done that since elementary school. After Global History, I went to Earth Science, Gym, Math, and after lunch, a double-period of English. I was done by 2 p.m.

Alyse was in all my classes except Gym and Math. She tried mad hard *not* to look at me, but I bet she was feeling me like I was feeling her. She had smooth, cocoa-brown skin, sweet pink lips, and a nice set of curves. The girl had style and class.

Too bad I wasn't looking for no girlfriend. If Young Drug Dealers of America were real, it would have a rule: *No girlfriends.*

Now I ain't saying no sex or no homegirls. But I think

anything that takes your attention off the business is dangerous.

My first girlfriend was a nut job named Tekeva. She spotted me one day in the park and put the word out that by the end of the day, I'd be hers. Tekeva had no problems getting me behind the clubhouse.

"Y'ever kissed before?" she asked me, hands on her hips.

"All the time." Inside, I was shaking, but on the outside I kept my cool. "You?"

"Son, I been tonguing since the fifth grade."

She didn't know that I *was* in the fifth grade.

"What's wrong with you, son? You shy or something?"

"Me?" No one ever called me shy before. I wasn't gonna let anybody do it now. I took a step closer.

She did the rest. Grabbing my skinny shoulders, she squeezed me tight. I got all excited, feeling her little tits rub against my chest and her grape bubblegum breath in my face.

She kissed me. I tilted her head just like I seen on TV. Then she went and ruined it by opening her lips so wide, I thought I'd fall in. Her tongue shot inside my mouth.

She pulled back. "Kiss me back, dumbass!"

"I ain't no dumbass. I'd kiss you back if you gave me the chance, bitch."

After that, she decided I was her man. She thought she could follow me anywhere she wanted, bug me while I was playing ball, and beat up any girl who talked to me.

When I realized that cursing her out and running away wasn't enough to get rid of her, I knew I had to do something. The problem? I didn't hit no girls. The solution? Pay a girl to do it for me.

My cousin Keyona was fifteen years old. We called her TLM: Tall, Lean, and Mean. She said the price of beating up Tekeva was three dinners at McDonald's. Three dinners! Since Keyona ate like a horse, that could be a lot of cash. So I got Keyona down to two dinners, and she kicked Tekeva's ass out of my life.

All my ladies since then was Tekevas. They wanted to be Queen of the Streets, and getting a piece of Ty Johnson was part of their master plan. Well, I told these girls I wasn't gonna be their ticket. If they wanted diamonds, go get a sugar daddy. And if they wanna get paid, go do some hustling.

You gotta be mad careful with women. Don't make promises you can't keep. You use the L word and they'll throw it back in your face. Mom is still going on about promises my dad made years ago.

Now I ain't saying that a young hustler can't ever have a girlfriend. But I say wait until you're twenty-one, get her tested for all the diseases you can think of *and* some shit you never heard of, and set her up right. When I'm twenty-one, I'll have time for a girlfriend. Until then, I'm staying away.

NOT ANOTHER DEAD WHITE GUY

TUESDAY I WENT TO MY FIRST TWO CLASSES, CUT OUT TO make a delivery, and came back for English. This school was supposed to be all that with its big alarmed doors and guards, but I knew its weak spot: the door behind the cafeteria used by the lunch workers.

English class was in a hot room in the basement with no windows. Ms. Amullo tried to make it brighter by putting posters over puke-yellow bulletin boards and fake flowers on her desk. Too bad it didn't work.

During the silent reading time, I put up my hand.

Ms. Amullo stopped beside me. "What can I do for you, Tyrone?"

"This play is mad boring. Don't you have something better than Shakespeare?"

"I'm afraid you'll have to live with it for the moment because it's required reading. But if you finish ahead of the class, you can use your silent reading time for something more interesting if you like. Do you see what Alyse is reading?"

Alyse, two seats ahead of me, was reading *The Bluest Eye*, by Toni Morrison.

"Is Toni Morrison another dead white guy?"

"Quite the opposite. She's a black woman, and very much alive."

"Hmm. Can I bring my own book?"

"That's fine, as long as I approve it first."

"Deal." I was gonna read the play fast, then use the silent reading time to read something good.

Before our reading time ended, I got through the first act.

Ms. Amullo said, "I'm handing out a poem by a British poet named Cameron Elsmore. I'd like you to analyze it in pairs. Alyse, will you work with Tyrone and show him how we analyze poetry?"

Alyse turned around. I winked.

Ms. Amullo went on. "Later I'll have a representative of each pair tell the class what you thought the poem was about, how it made you feel, and what stylistic devices you found. Now get started."

I moved my stuff to the desk behind Alyse, and she turned her desk around to face me. When Ms. Amullo put the paper between us, we both leaned over to read it, almost bumping heads.

She said, "Why don't you just read it to me, so I can get a first impression?"

"A'ight." I cleared my throat and read the poem, throwing in a little drama at different places.

"That's a beautiful poem," she said when I finished. "It has a lot of imagery. Thunderous skies. Wet, slippery grass."

"I know what you mean." Truth was, I was paying more attention to how I read than to what I read, so I didn't have a clue what the poem was about.

I reread it. "I like the part about the empty swings. Kinda like he misses being a kid, you know?"

She wrote that down. "Yeah, it was a good metaphor. There was a simile in there too. Something about the crash of thunder."

"'Thunder crashes, like cymbals clap.'"

"That's it."

I rocked back in my desk. "Go, girl. You dig this stuff?"

"Sure. I like to write free verse. You write poetry?"

"I been known to drop a rhyme."

"For real?"

"Uh-huh." I leaned closer to her. "You a brain. How'd you end up at this school?"

She sighed. "I . . . I been turning tricks for two years. I wanna get out of it. Make a new start."

I blinked. "You playing me?"

She burst out laughing. "I hope I don't look like a ho!"

"That was grimey."

She stared straight into my eyes. "I could ask you the same question, Ty. You wanna tell me what got you here?"

"Nah." I had a feeling that Alyse was the one girl in this school who wasn't gonna give me props for being a hustler. She was a square chick.

"Okay, so let's not swap stories about how we got here. Let's just make the best of it."

I nodded. "I like your style."

SPEAKING OF STYLE

AT 11:36 P.M., I GOT A CALL.

"Ty Johnson, my dog! Guess who's in town?"

I didn't have to guess. I knew.

Keron Maxwell. To rap fans, K-Ron—the biggest rap star to come out of BK since Jay-Z. Twenty-one years old and daddy of three (with three different babies' mamas), he was a hardcore gangsta rapper who made Usher look like a pussy and DMX like a cornball.

I knew K-Ron from the basketball courts down the block. I used to go there every day after school and not come home until Mom came looking for me. K-Ron would let me play with him and his friends—not out of charity. I was damn good for my age and cocky enough to say so. And when I started hooking him up with my daddy's product, well, we been tight ever since.

"K-Ron, what's good?"

"Bitches everywhere, that's what. Y'ain't seen nothing like it, dog! You gotta come help us out. And hook us up, while you at it."

"A'ight. Where you at?"

"The Wall. New club on—"

"I know where it is. I'll see you in a few."

Before hitting the shower, I called for a cab to pick me up in fifteen.

When he called I'd been lying on my bed, watching *The Wire* in my boxers, ready to turn in. But a smart businessman didn't pass up a chance to deal with K-Ron.

I put on new top-of-the-line white and black Rocawear. After spraying myself with Acqua di Gio, popping a gold stud in my ear, and throwing a gold chain around my neck, I walked out the door—quiet, since I didn't wanna wake the old lady.

A few minutes later I walked into The Wall like I owned the place. The bouncers recognized me and let me go by without any trouble. They knew Ty Johnson.

The air was smoky. The smell was sweat and perfume. K-Ron showing up made it official—this was the new hot spot.

I saw K-Ron and his crew before they saw me. Taking my time, I went to the VIP corner, where they were sitting in a leopard-skin booth. K-Ron was there with three homies and a bunch of girls looking like they charged by the hour. A girl with big shiny lips smiled at me. Hot thoughts went through my brain.

"Ty!" K-Ron leaned over and we slapped hands. He had more gold around his neck than an African prince.

"Sit down, my nigga!" K-Ron made the girls on his left clear out. "We celebrating. Just came from L.A. I finished the new—" He snapped his fingers at a waitress. "Get us another bottle of Cristal, sweet ass." He turned back to me. "I spent six weeks in the muthafucking studio. We making the first video next week. Wait till you see it! I'm'a be a priest."

"What twisted shit you up to now, K-Ron?"

"The track is called 'Sin.' In the video, you got this priest, and he be acting out the Seven Deadly Sins. It's gonna be hot! I'd ask if you wanna be an extra, but I know you got better ways to get paid. What you got for us tonight?"

"Premium from Bogotá." Under the table, I passed a little bag into his hands. He slipped it into the pocket of his jeans. "You like it, I'll bring more to your hotel tomorrow. You got my number."

I felt something soft bump against my leg. It was the shiny-lipped girl. She crossed her legs under the table, looking me up and down. "Hello."

"Holla, honey. What's your name?"

"Sherene."

"I'm Ty."

"I know. I heard you was coming."

K-Ron said, "Sherene's from L.A. She one of the models the priest be banging in the video." He leaned close to my ear. "She yours, Ty. I got my hands full."

I turned back to Sherene. "Hope your family ain't Catholic, Sherene."

"Who cares? They won't see the video."

The champagne came. K-Ron refilled his glass and passed the bottle around. Sherene sipped hers slow and sexy. I wasn't surprised when I felt her hand on my leg.

She squeezed. "Oohh. Somebody works out, don't he?"

"A man's body is his temple."

She touched my stomach. I flexed my six-pack. "Just how I like a brotha. Hard, in body and mind. I don't like no pushover." She flattened a hand on my chest. "I couldn't push you over if I tried."

"You welcome to try, shorty." I put a hand on her thigh.

She wasn't wearing stockings, so I felt the warm, soft skin. "Did I tell you that you got a hot body?"

Her fingers tickled behind my ear. "How can you say that if you don't really know?"

"Your dress don't leave much room for guessing."

Her lips touched my ear. "Do you wanna see for yourself?"

This girl didn't waste no time. She had her game on the minute I walked in. I bet she decided to fuck K-Ron's dealer no matter *who* he was. Anything to be a part of the posse, with all the bling and status that came with it. Whenever I saw K-Ron, he was surrounded by a dozen girls like her.

If a girl wanted to use me, it should at least be because of *my* reputation, not K-Ron's.

I said, "Thanks, but I got a girl."

"That don't matter to me."

"It should."

Her jaw dropped, and I saw a small retainer behind her bottom front teeth. I wondered how old—or how *young*—this girl really was.

K-Ron nudged me. "How's it going? We got extra rooms at the hotel, nigga."

"We don't need it."

"Come again?"

"I already got more chicks than I can handle."

"Amen, brotha! You smart to keep it under control. Can you believe I got another baby on the way? Now I got another baby's mama to deal with, and another baby's mama's mama." He started singing the OutKast song "Ms. Jackson": "Never meant to make your daughter cry / I apologize a trillion times."

That's K-Ron for you—wasn't gonna let a little thing like another baby get him down. "You the real deal, K-Ron."

"Fo sho." He slung an arm around me. "Yo, I got a proposal for you."

"Shoot."

"What would you say about taking a few months off and going on tour with me?"

"Bullshit."

"No bullshit. Here's how it's like, Ty. I try to get back to Brooklyn whenever I can, but most of the time I'm on the bus and in hotels. I need good people around me to keep it interesting. You, you keep it real, and you got mad style. I could use you."

Hmmm . . . limousines, chilling backstage, partying with rap stars . . .

"Man, I wish I could, but I gotta run my business."

"What about that nigga Sonny? Can't he hold shit down for you?"

I shook my head. "Business is hot right now. Would you take a break from rapping now that you on top? No way."

"You'll regret it for the rest of yo' life."

"Then I gotta live with that. I'll let you know if I change my mind."

"I know you, Ty. You ain't gonna change your mind."

"Maybe I will, maybe I won't."

"A'ight. But when you turn on the TV and see me on stage with 50 Cent or Diddy, you'll be one sorry-ass nigga."

"Whatever you say, K-Ron."

THIN ICE

THE NEXT MORNING THE DEAN CALLED ME INTO HIS OFFICE.

Dean Baxter was a family man, I saw from the pictures on his desk. He had three kids, and a wife with bleached blond hair and big, saggy tits. His shelves had fake-looking sports trophies, and the only thing on the wall was a poster of a runner crossing the finish line, arms in the air. The poster said: MOTIVATION + DETERMINATION = ACHIEVEMENT! The cheese made me wanna gag.

"Tyrone, I think you fail to understand the nature of this school. Yesterday you didn't show up to three of your classes, nor did you bring in a doctor's note to excuse your absence. Can you explain this blatant breach of our policy?"

"No." I yawned into my hand. I didn't get much sleep last night.

"I called your mother this morning to tell her you cut yester-day. I'm sure she'll have a word with you when you get home."

Shit.

"You find this funny, Mr. Johnson?"

"No." *I find this a complete waste of time.*

"Good."

He leaned over his desk. "Now tell me why you were cut-ting class."

"I made a mistake, sir."

"What were you doing?"

Dealing. "Working out."

"Working out?"

"Yeah."

"Why were you working out when you should've been in class?"

"A guy as tall as me gotta work out a lot if he don't want to lose muscle."

He stared at me. It was kind of fun seeing him so con-fused.

"Why couldn't you have worked out after school? We have a gym right here!"

"I got no excuse. Like I said, it was a mistake. Don't sweat it, sir. I'm gonna change." *From now on, whenever I cut* class, I'd cover my ass with a forged note. Mom would kill me if I got thrown out of here.

He slammed his hand on the desk. "He called me, you know."

"Who?"

"Your former guidance counselor, Mr. Edelstone. He told me about the games you play. He said you were very sly and you would make a lot of promises that you wouldn't keep."

Edelstone. Eddie, I liked to call him. Man, I missed playing that guy.

"I don't think you should judge me by the past," I said.

"Edelstone was right about one thing. You're a smooth talker. Head's up, Johnson. All your talk won't get you through another week at this school. You pull another stunt like you did yesterday, and you're out. I promise, you're going to look back twenty years from now as you're flipping burgers or cleaning toilets, and wish you hadn't been such an arrogant upstart."

"I hear you, Mr. Baxter. I'm gonna take this school more serious from now on. Thanks for the second chance." I got up.

He got up too. "It's not a second chance, Tyrone; it's a *last* chance. Is that clear?"

"Yeah."

AS IT COMES

"HEARD YOU MET WITH THE DEAN THIS MORNING."

"He was just blowing smoke."

Alyse and me paired up in English class again today. We had a term project to do, and I wasn't gonna do it with anybody else. She must've felt the same way, because the second Ms. Amullo told us to pair up, she turned to look at me.

"You better be careful," she said. "They're hardcore here. I don't want my partner getting kicked out before our project is finished."

"Then I guess I gotta stay in school until"—I looked at the project instructions—"until November sixth. That's about five weeks from now. I promise I won't get kicked out until then."

As she smiled at me, something vibrated against my leg.

It took me a second to realize it was my cell.

I checked the caller ID: *Clarissa 9-1-1.*

"I have to make a call." Raising my hand, I asked Ms. Amullo for the bathroom pass.

"Five minutes, Ty."

"I only need four."

I went around the corner to the boys' john and speed-dialed Clarissa's cell.

Static. *"Ty? Is this Ty?"*

"Clarissa? What's going on?"

"This ain't Clarissa. This is her best friend, Valerie. Clarissa's in the hospital. This bitch Sabrina was going around thinking she was the shit, flirting with Clarissa's man—"

"Yo, slow down. You telling me Clarissa got jumped?"

"Well, Clarissa came after her, but she had no choice, you know? She had to fuck her up since Sabrina tried to put the moves on her man. But Sabrina pulled out a razor and slashed her face."

"*Shit.* How bad is it?"

"She needed six stitches. Doc says there's gonna be a scar. Clarissa wanted me to call you 'cause she says you a good friend. She got no insurance. And her family, they got no money to cover the bills. She's all worried and upset. Clarissa ain't got a penny in the bank."

I groaned. Clarissa spent every cent she made on makeup, clothes, and magazines.

"Tell her I'll take care of it."

"Thank you, Ty! You so good to her."

"Sure." I clicked end. When the time was right, I'd have a talk with Clarissa about self-control.

I went back to class. Ms. Amullo opened the door for me.

"That was six minutes," she said.

"Ain't good to rush nature."

Hiding a smile, she let me go back to my seat.

"Some drama going on?" Alyse asked.

"*Women.*" And then, realizing what she might've thought, "Mom's always bugging about something."

"Speaking of women, I was thinking we could do Alice Walker for our project."

"Who's that?"

"She's a famous writer and feminist."

"Yo, I'd rather leave the feminists alone."

She rolled her eyes. "A feminist is just someone who believes in equal rights for men and women. Don't you believe in equal rights?"

Those eyes were so pretty but so damn serious.

"I ain't gonna sit here and say men and women are the same."

"It's not about being the *same*. It's about having the same rights. Shouldn't women get paid the same as men if they're doing the same work?"

"Yeah, I got no problem with that."

"Then you're a feminist too."

I laughed. "*Shit.* And I been walking around thinking all feminists were lesbians."

"That's B.S. Most lesbians are feminists, but most feminists aren't lesbians."

"Now I'm getting confused. Are you a lesbian or a feminist or both?"

"Would you like me less if I were a lesbian?"

"Depends. Could I join the action?"

"*Ty!*" She giggled.

"I'd still wanna be your partner for this project if you was a lesbian, don't worry. But . . . you ain't, right?"

She smiled. "That's for me to know and you to find out."

I was looking forward to finding out.

A MEETING WITH THE
PRINCE OF PAKISTAN

ONE OF MY HUSTLERS WAS A PAKISTANI KID NAMED MO. HE sold weed from the counter of the family deli, right under the nose of his clueless daddy. I wasn't sure if Mohammed was his first or last name, but I didn't really care.

Most of the time, I recruited peeps after watching them for a while, figuring out who they knew and how I could use them. Other times peeps came to me, wanting to get connected to my supply, or offering to work as a runner. Usually I turned them down. Put a few dollars in their pocket, they got cocky and started showing off. Po-po comes sniffing, and the trail leads back to me.

There were always exceptions. When Mo approached me a couple years back, I could tell the kid was the real deal. He wasn't looking to be big-time, he was just looking for a little cash. I had Monfrey watch him, make sure he wasn't a narc or a heavy user, before I agreed.

Mo worked the deli alone in the late afternoons, so I said I'd stop by Wednesday after school. A little bell above the doorway rang as I walked in. Behind the counter, a slick Pakistani guy served a couple of kids. I didn't know him.

I went to the back of the store, pretending to look at drinks, hoping I'd see Mo. I figured I could do a few minutes of hanging around before the guy at the counter got suspicious.

A minute later, Mo came out of a back room carrying some boxes. He saw me, then turned his back and started shelving the stuff.

I grabbed a soda, bought it at the counter, and went outside.

Mo kept me waiting ten minutes. We walked a block and turned a corner before he stopped. "Shit, that wasn't easy."

"Who's the guy?" I asked.

"My brother. He and his wife are down from Toronto."

That explained his Blue Jays jersey. I knew Mo wouldn't drop the cash for it himself. The kid never bought new clothes.

"Waqas's totally overdoing it," Mo said. "Whenever he comes to town he's breathing down my throat."

"Your neck."

"Whatever. He wants me to live and breathe that fucking store."

"Don't you?"

"Yeah, but he thinks I can always do more for the store, fix it up, work longer hours. *Dad is an old man now*, he always says. *You must do everything you can to help him.* Easy for him to say, living thousands of miles away." He looked up at me, realizing he was ranting about personal stuff that had nothing to do with me. "So, you got the stuff?"

We did the deal.

"A'ight, Mo. Call me with the next order. You gonna be able to hustle with your brother watching you so close?"

"Waqas has to go back to med school next week, so he'll be outta my hair."

"Your brother's in med school?"

"Uh-huh. He finishes this year. My father paid for the whole fucking thing."

"He can send your bro to med school with what he makes from that store?"

Mo nodded. "He's been saving since the day my brother was born. Too bad he can't afford to send me, too."

"You, in med school? You crazy?"

"Crazy? No way. I got the grades." He looked at me like *I* was crazy. "What do you think I been saving for?"

THE MAKING OF A HERO

ASK ANY BROTHER IN THE PROJECTS WHO HIS HERO IS, AND you'll hear the names of basketball and football players.

My hero was my dad. He was everything a man oughta be: strong, successful, smart. Men wanted to be his friend or they stayed away because they were afraid. Women couldn't get enough of him. He went to parent-teacher conferences just to hit on my teachers.

Orlando Johnson was raised by his grandma, dirt poor, in Prospect Heights. His mother died of a heart problem just after his brother Jean was born, and his father, well, he didn't know nothing about him, except that his father was better looking than Jean's. Grandma Johnson told him that much. She was a crabby old witch who was only good for one thing: bitching. She was too lazy to get off her saggy ass and get a job, but her nasty mouth wasn't too lazy to tell Orlando and Little Jean how she wished they was never born.

Orlando never knew a scrap of clothes that wasn't from the Salvation Army or a taste of meat that the butcher wasn't gonna throw out, anyway. Not until he started working for a family of Italian mafioso. Orlando learned all about Brooklyn's underworld. Strip clubs, brothels, weapons, drugs, there was nothing he wasn't into. And when Peter retired from the business, Orlando went out on his own.

Sure, he got caught. But in his day, he was king. He lived the American Dream. And once he got out, he'd be back on top again, with me by his side.

ORLANDO'S ONLY

THAT WEEK I GOT A POSTCARD.

Son,

Come see me this weekend.

Daddy O.

I got into Ossining on the noon train. It took half an hour to go through the paperwork and the searches. One guard liked frisking me a little too much, and I had to stop myself from smashing his ribs with my elbow.

As usual, the meeting was in the visitors' room. The plain white walls reminded me of the rehab center where we used to visit Uncle Jean. The difference was that this place had bars on the windows and guards at every exit.

I spotted my dad sitting at a back table.

"Hey, Dad."

"Son."

He clapped me hard on the back. This was the closest we ever got to hugging, and it was close enough for me.

Dad was looking good. He was mad brolic. Since he been in prison, he didn't have nothing else to do but work out. His head was shaved, and he had a goatee on his square chin. He wore a gold hoop in his left ear.

Leaning across the table, he grabbed my bicep, smiled. "You getting there. Got good genes after all."

"That's what they say."

"Family business still booming?"

Like he didn't know. Yo-yo prisoners and guards kept him up on things.

"You know it, Dad. Ain't no shortage of customers."

"Good." He sat back, folding his arms across his chest. "Proud of you, Ty. Sonny doing his job?"

"Yeah."

"I heard there was a fuck up with an undercover cop."

I nodded. "Sonny told you?"

"Nah, Sonny's too pussy to tell me that shit. Heard about it from a Brooklyn nigga last month. He said a boy named Michael Brown took the fall for a bigger operation. I remembered you telling me you got a kid named Michael Brown running errands."

"I had a bad feeling about it, so I told Sonny to send Michael."

Dad glared at me. "You should've listened to your instinct and sent nobody."

"I know. But Sonny was so sure about the guy. . . ."

"Sonny won't be making that kind of mistake again. When I found out about all this, I sent for him. We had a good talk."

"You probably had Sonny shitting his pants."

"I didn't take a whiff to find out. He knows I tell it to him straight. And he knows he wouldn't be nothing without me."

"Me, too, Dad."

"You better believe it. What would you be doing now if you wasn't running the family business, huh? Working at McDonald's?" He grinned. "You owe me, son. You better be around to buy me diapers when I'm eighty and can't hold my piss."

"I'll buy you diapers and pay some hot young chick to put 'em on you."

We laughed.

"I also wanted to tell you, Ty, that you don't have to worry about Michael Brown slipping up."

"What do you mean?"

"I took steps to make sure he don't talk."

"What kinda steps?"

"I got connections in juvey. They making sure he keeps his mouth shut."

My hands made fists under the table. "Dad, keep them away from Michael Brown. He just a kid, loyal as hell. Ain't no snitch."

"Chill, a'ight? I'm just taking precautions. Michael Brown knows he'll get seriously fucked up if he talks."

"Dad, look. When I need your help, I'll ask for it. I ain't asked for it in a while. I'm holding shit down."

"No need to get salty, Ty. You your own man now. I ain't doubting that."

"Good." I told myself to chill. Dad was locked up, for Christ's sake. I was the one making the calls on the street, not him. If he got some satisfaction out of butting his nose in, fine. Reality was, Orlando wasn't up for parole for another three years.

I decided to change the topic. "So, how's Reg and Midas?"

"Missing their hos."

"Too bad they ain't got girls like Lorraine."

He smiled. "Yeah, she one fine woman. She was here last week."

Lorraine was in Dad's life for as long as I could remember. On the outside, she was just one of his girlfriends. Since he got put away, she was the only one. Calling herself Orlando's almost-wife, she strutted the streets thinking she was big-time.

"What about you, Ty? How are the ladies?"

"K-Ron was in town last week. We had some wild times."

Dad smacked his hand on the table. "Bet you did! D'you know, I tell the niggas in here that my son be friends with K-Ron, and some don't even believe it?"

"They just jealous."

THE CASE OF THE JAMAICAN MUSHROOMS

I USED TO BELIEVE IN TRYING EVERYTHING ONCE.

That was before I tried Cheddar's Jamaican mushrooms.

By the time I was fourteen, I was a hardcore hustler. But I wasn't tempted to start using. I knew too many people who lost everything to drugs, like my uncle Jean.

Still, Dad always said that a man should try everything once, and the wannabe Original Gangsta that I was, I thought maybe he was right.

So when Cheddar met me in the park with these Jamaican mushrooms he got from his cousin, I said we'd split them.

"This shit is sour." I downed them fast. "They'd be better with ketchup. We should've gone to McDick's and mixed 'em with our fries."

"I should've put some in Mom's chicken stew!"

"You think cooking with these would make them stronger or weaker?"

He shrugged.

"Well, heat evaporates stuff, right? So maybe weaker. I'll ask Ms. McEvoy on Monday."

Cheddar's eyes bugged out. "You seriously gonna ask Ms. McEvoy?"

"Hell, yeah. She get paid to answer our questions, don't she?"

"She'll tell Guidance if you ask her."

"So?" I wrinkled my nose. "I don't think these 'shrooms is working. I think your cousin played us."

"Rodney don't joke about drugs or sports. Just wait. By the time the homies show up, we'll be all fucked up and they'll be jealous. You think Kim will be at the dance?"

"Her mom's strict. Makes her sing in the church choir. I don't know if she'll let her go."

"She better be there. She's so hot." He leaned forward, staring down at his lap.

"Cool it down, Cheddar. I can see you sweating. Save it for the bedroom, son."

"It ain't that. My head's feeling weird." He turned to me, his eyes bloodshot. "Your head feel weird?"

"You imagining things. Ain't nothing in these damn 'shrooms. I hope you didn't give Rodney no money."

"Nah. No money." He looked past me and waved. "There's Joe and Bear."

Joe Joseph was always rocking the phatest gear. But his parents must've been on Jamaican mushrooms when they named him.

Bear didn't get his name from being big; it was because his last name was Beardsley. His first name was Keith. A quiet brother, Bear was okay with being the butt of our jokes because we let him hang around with us young OGs.

Both of my boys were styled up for the dance, Joe's gear yellow and black, Bear's gray and red. I wished Joe had shared a few sprays of his Drakkar Noir with Bear.

We all pounded palms.

"Sorry, niggas, you too late," Cheddar said. "Missed all the magic mushrooms."

"You serious?" Joe looked at me. "Ty, you got enough for us, right?"

"They wasn't mine."

"Huh?"

"Cheddar got connections too."

"That ain't fair." Joe glared at us.

Cheddar and me laughed.

"This shit is strong!" Cheddar hyped.

"Mad strong!" I crossed my eyes, even though I didn't really feel nothing.

Joe said, "C'mon, homeboy junkies, we better get going. Doors close at nine."

We headed to the school. Seeing three seventh-grade girls, we walked a few feet behind them. As I stared at their fine little asses, my eyes started to blur, like bad reception on my grandma's old TV. I clapped a hand on Joe's shoulder. "This is hard shit, Joe."

"Serves you right for not sharing."

I looked over at Cheddar. He looked good, head up high, smile on his face. Problem was, there was two of him.

"Cheddar! Who's your twin?"

"What the fuck you talking about?"

"Ha! I'm tripping! I'm baked as a fucking cake!"

"You ain't the only one, nigga!"

Joe said, "You two better start acting normal if you wanna get into the dance."

"No sweat. Right, Cheddar? We can act normal."

"*No problemo, muchacho!*"

Kids lined up at the front doors of the school. We were at the end of the line, right behind the cute seventh graders.

"Ladeez, how you doing?" Cheddar slurred.

"Uh, good." The girls started giggling.

"Tits, nice tits," *even if there was four of them.* Her tits were winking at me, ready to pop out like little rockets.

"*Ty,*" Joe said, glaring at me with a thousand eyeballs. "Chill."

I felt a shove against my shoulder. "Don't you talk to my friend that way." Tits's friend Red Shirt was all up in my face. "Show some respect for a sista, dumbass!"

Everybody went, "Ohhhh . . ."

Joe grabbed my arm. "Let it go, Ty."

"Let what go? We gonna dance or what?"

"What, you turned faggot on me now?"

"Faggot? Huh? Dance . . . dance." I heard music blaring inside. "Dance inside!"

"Yeah." He whispered, "You lucky that girl backed down, son. You don't wanna have to hit no girl."

I wasn't listening.

I blew through the metal detectors and got a pat-down from a she-man guard. Joe stayed close so I didn't give anyone lip.

We got into the building, no problem. But when we went into the dance, the loud music and flashing lights made my head spin.

I put my hands over my ears.

I was shaking. Somebody was shaking me.

"Ty, Ty! Keep it together man! We gonna get thrown out!"

I opened my eyes. Joe. Trying to talk to me. Weird mouth sounds.

Lights flashed.

My body spazzed. My mind screamed.

Hands grabbed at me. Hands turned into snakes. Fought them as hard as I could.

I blacked out.

Hospital. Choking. Stomach on fire. Can't breathe.

Morning. I woke up in a bedroom plastered with basketball posters. It wasn't my bedroom. It was Joe Joseph's.

For a whole minute I stared at a poster of Michael Jordan, his tongue hanging out as he went for a slam dunk. I started to remember last night.

The girls.

The dance.

The hospital.

Holy shit.

How the hell was I gonna leave this room and face Joe's family?

There was a knock at the door.

Joe came in. "How you feeling?"

"Okay. Why am I here? I don't . . ."

"The hospital called your place. Your mom wasn't there, so mine came. Cheddar and Bear, they took off when the ambulance showed up."

In their shoes, I would've done the same. It was strange that Joe didn't.

"I bet your mom freaked out," I said.

"Yeah, well."

"Look, I'll tell her you wasn't doing 'shrooms. I'll talk to her." I didn't know *how* I'd do that. Joe's mom was a church lady. Church ladies scared me.

"It's all right. She believed me. You can come into the kitchen and eat something."

"No thanks. I gotta get home." I swung my legs out of bed. "Does my mom know I'm here?"

"Yeah. Mom called and left a message."

"Shit. Well, I'll deal with her. Did the cops come?"

"No. We got you outta the gym through the fire exit, then called the ambulance from a payphone. You was tripping, Ty. I thought maybe you'd . . . die, you know?"

"Ah shit, son. Nobody dies from a few 'shrooms."

Joe sighed. "Whatever."

"C'mon, man, don't be like that. Think of how it all went down! No cops, no trouble with the school, no nothing! I can still talk to your mom—"

"Don't sweat it."

"A'ight. I'll call you later. I owe you big, son. We'll go see a movie. It's on me, playa!"

"Don't call. My mom . . ."

The look on his face said it all.

Control wasn't all I lost that night. Joe's parents wouldn't let him hang out with me no more.

One good thing came out of it: I learned never to give up control again. Not for a day, an hour, a minute.

And I learned that the idea of trying everything once is bullshit.

GIRLS, LIKE BASKETBALL

TONIGHT WAS THE NIGHT.

I caught the elevator to the eighth floor, feeling something weird in my stomach. Damn, was I sweating over a girl?

Well, Alyse wasn't the type of girl I was used to. She lived in the hood, but she was no hood rat. You could tell just by looking at her that she lived clean. And when you talked to her, you knew she was mad smart.

But this was no date, I told myself. She only invited me over to work on our project. And I wasn't looking for no girl-friend, anyway.

That didn't mean we couldn't enjoy what Mama Nature gave us, if she was up for it.

The way I saw it, girls were like basketball, and I knew how to *swish*.

I knocked on the door. I heard music inside. A bass line of African drums.

I heard feet moving, then the door handle turned.

"Hi." In a red shirt and tight blue jeans, she looked so fine. She was wearing a little more makeup than usual, and some perfume. I could tell that she was a little nervous.

"Come in. Sorry it's kinda messy."

"Any cozy crib is kinda messy," I said, though my own crib was neat as hell.

I heard a noise behind her. A little kid in overalls was trying to fit a toy into his mouth.

"Don't do that!" Alyse took the toy away from him. "*No, sweetie.*" The kid plopped down on his butt and giggled.

"What's his name?"

"Gavin."

"Hey, Gavin. What up, G?" I bent down and patted his head. "He your brother?"

"He's my son." She didn't look at me.

That knocked the wind right out of me. I couldn't think of what the hell to say except, "He's cute."

"Thanks."

"Uh, how old is he?"

"Almost two."

"His daddy around?"

"His daddy isn't in my life. We live with my mom."

"Oh."

"Guess you weren't expecting this." It sounded like she was apologizing.

"Ain't nothing. Lots of girls I know got babies. This ain't nineteen fifty-three."

"You looked surprised."

"Me? Nah."

She patted Gavin's stomach, making him giggle and try to grab her hands. "The first year, I stayed home with him. Then Mom found a job where she could do evening shifts, so she's home while I'm at school."

"That works."

"Yeah. Anyway, let's get started. We can work at the kitchen table. That way, we can spread our stuff out and I can still keep an eye on Gavin."

We sat down at the table. A lot about Alyse was now making sense. Maybe being a mom was why she acted so much like an adult.

"Ty, did you hear what I said?"

"Uh, no, sorry."

"I asked if you have Internet access at home."

"Yeah, I use it all the time." I wrote my screen name on a piece of paper and passed it to her.

"Your IM is 'King of Streets'?" She laughed. "That's a good one. I'm Alyseinwonderland."

"I like it."

"Thanks. Now, I was thinking that if we use two Internet sources and three books for the project, that should be enough."

"We don't gotta O.D. We can get all we need in one book."

"Yeah, but we want to show Ms. Amullo that we looked at a few different sources. We'll look them over, even if we don't actually use them all. I want to get an A on this."

"I can't even remember the last time I got an A."

"Really? That's weird. I mean, you're such a smart guy, I don't think it would take much for you to get A's."

"To get A's, you gotta go to class. I ain't good at that."

"Don't you want to get into a good college?"

"I don't need college. I'm gonna start my own business right out of high school."

"Don't you need money to start a business?"

I couldn't tell her that I already had plenty. "Don't worry, Alyse. I got a business plan."

"If I were you, I'd get the best marks I can in high school, just in case your plans fall through. As for me, I have to get A's if I'm going to college." She looked at her son. "Eventually . . . I'll get where I want to be."

"Where's that?"

"A criminal lawyer."

"So you gonna put the bad guys away, or help them get off?"

"I'll be a prosecutor. I want to get criminals off the streets."

"I'd'a thought you'd be a defense attorney."

"Defense? Sure, I'd defend an *innocent* person. But I don't want to make my living helping good-for-nothing murderers or rapists or drug dealers get off easy."

Since when were hustlers as bad as murderers and rapists? I decided to be smart and keep my mouth shut.

An hour and a half later, when Alyse was sure that we'd done enough work, we decided to watch some BET. She'd already put Gavin to bed, so it was just gonna be us.

Alyse went into the kitchen to make some microwave popcorn, so I got up from the table and went over to the couch. I plunked down. My ass hit something hard. The couch spring was broken. I scooted around till I got comfortable.

Alyse came back with a bowl of popcorn and two Cokes on a tray. By that time, I had on *The Bernie Mac Show*.

She sat down on the couch, not too close, but not too far. The broken spring did me a favor, tilting her my way.

"You like Bernie Mac?" I asked.

"Yeah."

"It's a good show. But I hear his stand-up's better." I ate some popcorn. "The best is Chris Rock's stand-up, though. I saw him last year in the city. It was hot. But a little nasty." I looked down at her. "That stuff bother you?"

"Not if it's funny. But nasty and not funny, that's the worst."

"Word."

After Bernie Mac, we watched the end of a music awards show hosted by some skinny white guy I never heard of. I liked chilling with her and hearing what she had to say on a lot of things.

At one point she turned to me with a big smile. "You know, I'm glad you came to Les Chancellor. Classes are more interesting with you there."

I smiled back. "We have a good time, don't we?"

"The best." Her eyes sparkled, and I could tell she was feeling me.

My cell phone rang. *Fuck it, I won't answer.* But Alyse had already looked away.

I flicked it open. The caller ID said: *Monfrey*.

I answered, "Yeah?"

"Ty, we might have a problem."

"Go on."

"There are new niggas in the hood. They're asking too many questions."

"Like what?"

"Like who the connections are."

"So?"

"Well, it ain't that I think they're narcs. I never seen narcs who look *that* much like thugs. I just got a bad feeling about them."

"Then go with your gut. I hope you and Davica can work it out."

"Huh? Oh shit, someone's there, right?"

"Bingo. I gotta go, man."

"Okay. I wanted to give you the heads-up."

"Gotcha. Later, man." I hung up.

"Is everything all right?"

"Yeah. It's this friend of mine. He got girl problems."

She smiled. "That's cute that he calls you for advice."

"He trifling, that's what. He always got drama going on."

"I got friends like that too." She yawned. I knew what that was. It was the dismissal bell.

I took a deep breath, staring into that pretty face. This thing between us was really something. And if we didn't do nothing about it tonight, it was definitely gonna be there tomorrow.

THE CODE OF THE WARRIOR

BY MID-OCTOBER, I WAS FINDING MY GROOVE. IT WAS MAD HARD not cutting class, but I knew the second I slipped up, I'd get kicked out.

It didn't hurt that I had Alyse to hang with. She was so cute, I did *homework* so that I could be with her. Sometimes I even studied for tests, just to see if I could get a better mark than her.

And sometimes class was kinda interesting too.

Like Global History. Boring, right?

Today was different.

Mr. Guzman was looking down at his notes, rubbing his hands together. When the bell rang, his head snapped up. "Good morning! I'm going to start us off with a question that relates to our new unit. What are the qualities of a great warrior?"

I raised my hand. "He's physically and mentally strong.

He can lead an army or take orders if he got to. He ain't afraid of nothing."

"What about his mind-set going into battle? What should it be?"

Justin answered, "He should be calm."

"He gotta keep his eye on his goal and nothing else," I added.

"Well, have any of you heard of samurai warriors?" Mr. Guzman asked.

Someone called out, "Yeah, they those guys in black who do karate."

"You might be talking about ninjas, but the idea isn't dissimilar." Mr. Guzman wrote on the board, *Bushido: the Way of the Warrior*. "Bushido is the code of conduct of the samurai warrior. In medieval Europe, the knights also had a code. It was called chivalry. But in Japan, Bushido was different. In Bushido, you trained all your life for battle, and when you went into battle, you went in seeking to die."

"That's stupid," Richard said. "If you go in thinking you gonna die, then you'll die for sure."

"The idea is that if you don't fear death—and in fact, expect and welcome it—you will be a better soldier," Mr. Guzman said. "A killing machine."

Alyse said, "I guess they thought that since they were going to die, anyway, they might as well do it bravely, and take down as many enemies as they could."

"But what's the point in being a hero if you dead?" Kristina asked. "Sorry, but that don't make sense."

"Maybe they promised the samurais forty virgins when they die," Todd said. "Like those terrorists."

Mr. Guzman said, "It could be they were promised rewards in the afterlife. Or perhaps death itself was their honor."

"It's like those kamikaze pilots during World War Two," Alyse said. "Or the 9/11 hijackers."

"This is wack, if you ask me," I said. "Those samurais should've stood up for themselves. It's stupid to give up your life just because your leader tells you to. Most leaders stay safe while they send their men to die."

Alyse nodded. "Like President Bush sending soldiers into Iraq."

"Maybe that's why it's called *Bush*-ido," I said.

Everybody laughed, even Mr. Guzman.

From there, the class went on about life in early Japan, feudalism, and all that. Mr. Guzman always hooked us in with something interesting, then switched over to what he really wanted to teach.

I couldn't concentrate on the rest of the lesson because my mind kept going back to Bushido, the way of the warrior. That whole thing was ass-backward. I knew that a great warrior wasn't supposed to be scared of death. But asking for death as part of the warrior's path? That was overdoing it.

JIMMY PENNINGTON: THE WHITE, IVY LEAGUE VERSION OF MO

I GAVE PROPS TO JIMMY PENNINGTON. HE WAS A WALL STREET broker who sold coke as easy as he sold stocks. For the past year he been dropping fifty Gs a month—a hot deal for both of us.

Tonight he wanted seventy-five. I carried it in a briefcase as I walked into his favorite TriBeCa after-work lounge.

Jimmy sprawled in a cushy chair near the front of the lounge, staring out the window at passing people. He wasn't into making deals at shady places like piers or parking lots. He liked to meet in upscale places. All I had to do was throw on some dress shoes and pants, a white button-down shirt, and a leather jacket and I was good to go.

"Hi, Jimmy."

"Johnson!" He got up, shook my hand, and clapped my back. "Great to see you. How's law school?"

He was always saying things like that. "Top of my class." I sat down and put the briefcase under the table.

"That's some achievement, Johnson. Drinks on me." He flagged down the waitress. "Two martinis, extra olives."

Jimmy dragged the briefcase close to him. "All here?"

"You got it."

"Excellent." He leaned back in his chair like a young Donald Trump—with better hair. Jimmy dropped thousands on threads: Armani suits and loafers, engraved cufflinks. For a guy in his mid-twenties he had it all, but Jimmy always wanted more.

"Got some new connections, do you?" I asked.

"Sure have, Johnson. Give it a little time, and I'll be asking you for a hundred every month."

"Whatever you need. Just call."

Jimmy laughed. "Like the God-damned Visiting Nurse Service of New York!"

I took my martini from the waitress. The service was fast, but I wasn't surprised that Jimmy got special service. He gave out phat tips.

I sipped the martini. It was so damn sour. Jimmy put them down like Gatorade.

"You still with that lawyer?" I asked.

He smiled. "Woman of my dreams. Just moved in with me."

"Sounds serious."

"Sure is. I'm sick of the bar scene. I've got a gorgeous woman who's great in bed and makes almost as much as I do. Plus, she works late, so we don't get on each other's nerves."

"Does she know about . . ."

"She's a practicing Catholic, for Christ's sake. The other week she dragged me to Mass. I told her next week I'd go to confession. I'm going to enjoy spilling my guts."

"Maybe you taking the joke a little far, man."

He waved it off. "Priests can't do anything with what we tell them, trust me. I'm sure the priest'll just tell me to stop selling, say a few Hail Marys, and move on." He flashed a smile, then gulped more martini. "You should go sometime, eh, Johnson? I bet you have a few sins to confess."

"It don't matter. I'm Presbyterian."

"Amen." We clanked glasses.

CYBER CHAT

ALYSEINWONDERLAND: IS THAT YOU, TY?

I blinked at the instant message that popped up on the screen. I'd spent the last hour surfing for sports news and porn, and now I suddenly woke up.

King_of_Streets: Maybe. Who wants to know?

Alyseinwonderland: Can't you tell? Just tell me your last name and I'll know whether to keep on chatting with you.

King_of_Streets: What are you wearing, honey?

Alyseinwonderland: Ty! Stop playing.

King_of_Streets: Maybe you're confusing me with King_of_*the*_Streets.

Alyseinwonderland: Am I?

King_of_Streets: That's for me to know and you to find out.

Alyseinwonderland: Ha! :) I heard that before. So it *is* you, Ty. You threw me off for a minute there.

King_of_Streets: A man's gotta have a little fun.

Alyseinwonderland: Oh, we're a man now, are we?

King_of_Streets: What, I ain't old enough to be a man?

Alyseinwonderland: I wouldn't say that. Being a man really isn't about age. It's about taking responsibility, isn't it?

King_of_Streets: I forgot I was talking to Oprah Winfrey.

Alyseinwonderland: Actually, this is Iyanla. She's just as wise as Oprah.

King_of_Streets: Never heard of her.

Alyseinwonderland: Pick up *Essence* magazine to find out, or go to a bookstore.

King_of_Streets: Sorry, shorty. I got better things to do than read that stuff.

Alyseinwonderland: And I guess you read *National Geographic*?

King_of_Streets: Damn straight. It's got hot pictures of naked women in the Amazon and all that sh (*backspace*) stuff.

Alyseinwonderland: You just stopped yourself from cursing, didn't you?

King_of_Streets: Of course. Wouldn't wanna curse in front of a lady, would I?

Alyseinwonderland: Real smooth, Ty. You won't curse, but you admit you read *National Geographic* for the naked women.

King_of_Streets: What can I say? ;)

Alyseinwonderland: Hey, what about coming over to do some work on our project Saturday night?

King_of_Streets: You wanna study on a Saturday night? What about letting me take you out?

Alyseinwonderland: I can't leave Gavin.

King_of_Streets: I'll get you a babysitter.

Alyseinwonderland: That's sweet of you to offer, but it's too much money. How about we study and then I cook you dinner? I make a mean spaghetti. Then later you can meet up with your friends or whatever.

King_of_Streets: Forget my friends. We'll do a little work, have dinner, then rent a movie.

Alyseinwonderland: Sounds perfect. Thanks . . . you're a really good guy.

King_of_Streets: No, I ain't. But I'm a guy who thinks you're . . .

Alyseinwonderland: What???

King_of_Streets: . . . different from any girl I know.

Alyseinwonderland: Is that a good thing??

King_of_Streets: For you or for me?

Alyseinwonderland: Both.

King_of_Streets: Yeah, it is.

Alyseinwonderland: Thank you, Your Majesty.

King_of_Streets: No, thank *you*, Alyse.

Alyseinwonderland: Good night.

King_of_Streets: Sweet dreams.

We both logged off. I sat there for a while, staring at the computer screen.

Something was starting between me and Alyse. Something real.

THE DATE

I KNOCKED ON HER DOOR AT 8 P.M. SHARP, ROCKING phat gear with everything—jersey, pants, socks, watch, and do-rag—matching perfect. I topped it off with an expensive diamond and sapphire earring I bought last week.

No way she wouldn't think I was fly.

The door swung open.

The air whooshed out of my lungs. Lord, I never seen anything so fine in my life.

This wasn't the jeans-and-T-shirt Alyse I was used to. She just cranked herself up from pretty to gorgeous. She wore a tight pink tank top under a black jacket, and a matching miniskirt showing off two of the finest legs I ever seen. On her feet she wore black heels. Her jewelry was dangly and gold. Her lips were shiny and pink. I was gonna kiss those sweet lips if it was the last thing I did.

"Alyse, you sooo fine."

She smiled. "Thanks. Come in."

I followed her in, almost dropping to my knees and begging for mercy when I saw how good she was looking round back in that skirt.

We went into the kitchen, where she poured me some orange soda.

"I know I promised to make you dinner, but I thought we could go out instead. Gavin's sleeping over at a friend's."

"Two-year-olds is going to sleepovers now?"

"His mom's my neighbor and a good friend. Maria's always offering to take him for a night, you know, so I can have a life."

"Nice lady."

"Yeah. So"—she looked down at the books and papers on the kitchen table—"we'll do this another time?"

"Sure."

She grabbed her coat and pocketbook, and we left the apartment. In the elevator, she said, "I've got a two-for-one coupon for an Italian place on Court Street."

"Save the coupon for another time. I got somewhere in mind. You got your MetroCard with you?"

"Yeah, why?"

"'Cause I'm taking you into the city."

Her mouth opened like she was gonna ask where, but then she closed it. I think she liked surprises. I was hyped to see the look on her face when she saw where I was taking her.

We hopped the 2 train into Manhattan, riding it for half an hour to Columbus Circle. After walking three blocks, we were at Chez Gigi.

She stayed back. "This place looks expensive. Maybe we should go somewhere else."

"I been here before. The food is the best. It's on me, Alyse."

"But—"

"Come on. I promise you ain't gonna regret it."

"Well . . . okay."

I opened the door for her.

She looked around at the classy place. "You sure about this?"

"Don't I look sure?" I turned to the slick-haired maître d'. "For two, please."

"Follow me, monsieur, madame."

I had to tug Alyse's hand to make her follow the maître d' to the table. When we sat down, the maître d' handed us a wine list and two menus. "Your waiter will be with you momentarily."

"Thank you," I said.

"This is the most beautiful restaurant I've ever seen, Ty!"

"Trust me, once you taste the food, you'll know why this restaurant is so famous."

"It's famous? Wait till I tell Maria. She won't believe it!" Opening the menu, I saw her excitement die. "This is way too much. I can't let you do this. We can still leave, since we haven't ordered anything."

I took her hand. "I told you before that I work part-time at the gym. I wanna make the most of my money. Don't you think everybody should live the good life sometimes?"

"I guess so, if you're sure. . . ." She squeezed my hand.

"What do you say we order some wine?" I put the wine list in front of her. "Your choice, shorty."

She leaned forward and whispered, "You think they'll let us order wine?"

"Hell, yeah. Places like this don't ask for I.D., and they don't give you the check until you ask for it."

"Sounds like you have a lot of experience with places like this."

"Nah. Now choose us a wine, will ya?"

She looked down at the wine list. "I don't know much about wine, but I think I like red best. I had some at my grandparents' last Christmas, and it was great. It might've been . . . merlot?"

"Merlot, you got it. Which merlot?"

"Hmmm . . . There are a million here. French, Australian, Californian . . . I want something exotic. How about South African?"

"I hear that. For Mother Africa."

The waiter came, and I ordered the wine. When the waiter said, "Excellent choice," I winked at Alyse.

We took our time, studying the menu like we were cramming for an exam.

"What's foie gras, Ty?"

"It's good stuff. We'll get some."

"But what does it mean?"

"Duck fat."

"You serious?"

"Don't I look serious?"

"I don't know. You always say, 'Don't I look serious?' But deep down, I think you're laughing."

"You think I'm laughing at you?"

"No, not at me. At everything. It's like you know the punch line to a joke and you're not telling. You've got this—this mystery about you."

The side of my mouth went up. "I do?"

"Am I right or am I right?"

"Are you ever wrong?"

"That's you being mysterious again!"

"You like it when I'm mysterious?"

"It's not the mystery I like, it's you." She looked away, embarrassed. "What I mean is, you're a cool guy, you know?"

"I better be if I'm here with you."

We looked at each other. Whoa.

The waiter came back, pouring each of us a glass of wine. We picked them up for a toast.

"What should we toast?" she asked.

"To making more money than we could ever spend."

She laughed. "Be serious!"

I *was* serious. But, instead, I said, "To a happy life."

She clinked my glass. "To a happy life."

• • •

The meal was da bomb. I never had so much fun with a girl. Our conversation flowed like the wine we were drinking. And her beauty blew a brother away. Most ghetto girls didn't have the class for a place like Chez Gigi. But Alyse was Park Avenue all the way.

Feeling full and a little drunk, we headed back to Brooklyn. Back at her place, we sat on the couch and put on MTV.

Putting an arm around her, I leaned back into the couch, smiling to myself. A well-trained athlete knew his game, and when it was time to shoot from the three-point line, a real playa couldn't miss.

I tucked a curl behind her ear, stroking two fingers down the curve of her cheek to her chin. She made a little noise and moved closer to me, laying her head on my chest. I lifted her chin until she was looking in my eyes, and kissed her.

She stiffened at first, but gradually she relaxed and kissed me back, nice and slow. I deepened the kiss. When our tongues touched, we both moaned.

She pulled her lips away, and my mouth moved across her face. I whispered in her ear, "You so sexy, boo."

"Thanks . . . It's pretty late."

I pulled back so I could look at her face. "You're right. Maybe it's time . . ." *for us to go to bed.* But I could see in her eyes that she didn't want me to say it. For her, me leaving now would be a perfect ending to the night. And even though my body was fired up, I didn't want to disappoint her. "Maybe it's time for me to go."

"I think so too."

I stepped into the hallway. She took my hand. "Thank you, Ty. This was the greatest night I've had in a long time. It was wonderful."

"You made it wonderful." I bent down and kissed her.

"See you Monday." Giving me a little wave, she closed the door.

On the cab ride home, I leaned my head against the leather seat, closed my eyes, and wished that Alyse was in my arms again. I could still smell her perfume, still taste those soft lips. . . .

My cell phone rang. I was so sure it was Alyse calling to whisper in my ear, I didn't even check the caller ID. "Hello."

"Ty? That you?" Sonny's voice.

"It's me."

"Damn, boy, haven't you been checking your messages?" His shouting couldn't cover up the shakiness in his voice. "Carlos got jumped. He's hurt real bad. We got people tryna bring us down. I don't know what the fuck they'll do next!"

"Sonny, calm down." I told the cabbie, "Take a right at the next light. We going to East Flatbush—13 Mulgrew Place." Into the phone I said, "Hang on, Sonny. I'm coming over."

THE COMPETITOR

GIVING THE DRIVER HIS CASH, I RAN INSIDE THE BUILDING and hit the button. Sonny buzzed me up. He was standing in the doorway of his apartment in sweat pants and a wife-beater. "Get in here."

The apartment was huge, with sleek tiled floors, leather couches, and a hot entertainment system. I barely sat down when Sonny said, "Carlos got jumped tonight when he was making deliveries. They fucked him up, took the stuff, and made him cough up the names of the customers he was delivering to."

"You talked to Carlos?"

"No, his girl called me. Them bitches who messed him up told him to give us a message: 'Darkman's in town and he's shutting us down.'"

"Darkman? He some sorta comic character?"

"Whoever the fuck he is, he knows who we are. Carlos can't hold in a fucking fart."

"*Shit*, I got warned about this."

"Huh? Who warned you?"

"Monfrey. Said there was some shady niggas around. I didn't take him serious."

I was all about Alyse then, I remembered. *Damn*, I was right that women were a distraction.

I said, "Anybody new in the hood can tell that Carlos is probably running for someone. That skinny cat ain't sly. So we don't know how much Darkman knows about us. He could've been lying low for weeks, getting ready to strike."

I heard Sonny swallow.

"We gonna hold it down," I said. "First thing we have to worry about is that he knows the names of some customers. He might try to sweet-talk them into buying from him. We gotta get to them first and let 'em know we still the best deal in town."

"I been all over that. Carlos's girl told me the names of the three customers he gave up, and I spoke to them. They'll get their next hit half price. We cool with them."

"Good, you stay on it. We have to remind our peeps that we still their number one. Keep 'em happy. I'll deal with the other side of this. I'm gonna find out who this Darkman is."

"And then what?"

"We wait for him on the battlefield."

I didn't have to open up Sun Tzu's *The Art of War* to figure out what to do about Darkman. I'd lived and breathed that book for years.

> *Knowledge of the enemy's dispositions can only be obtained from other men.*
>
> *It is always necessary to begin by finding the names of the attendants, aides, the door-keepers, and sentries of the general in command. We must commission spies to discover these.*

I found Rob Monfrey the next morning on a park bench, smoking up.

"Ty, what it be like?"

"We got trouble." I scanned the bench for bird shit and sat down.

"I know. Heard they fucked up Carlos."

"Uh-huh. Tell me everything you know about this Darkman."

"All I know is, he used to run a big-time operation down in Miami. Don't know why he came up here. The guys working for him, they from Miami too."

"I hope he bought them return tickets. They try to sell to you?"

"Yeah, last night. One of 'em saw me smoking. Asked where I got the stuff. Said I found it in a mailbox. He said he'd sell me some real cheap. I told him I don't smoke regular like. He said, 'Yeah, right,' and walked away."

"I like how you handled that. But next time, do it different. If you stay visible, one of those guys is gonna approach you again. Let 'em know you can't afford to pay for no weed. But if they need shit done, you can swing that."

"Sounds like you asking me to be a spy." Monfrey grinned. "I like it, son."

"Make yourself mad helpful to them. I want you to find out everything you can about their leader and their operation. Find out Darkman's real name, how many men he got working for him, where he goes to eat—anything."

"Easy peasy."

"You a natural, Monfrey, but these guys are dangerous. If

you think they suspect you, get away from them fast—got that?"

"I got you."

"You can name your price for this job."

"PlayStation 3?"

That was the thing about Monfrey. He had no fucking idea how much he was worth.

"PlayStation 3, ten of the hottest games, and a pair of Jordans. How about that?"

He slapped my hand. "We got a deal."

I didn't go to school on Monday. No time. I had to secure my ops, and that meant talking to every member of my team, from the big players to the small-time runners, to make sure there weren't any cracks.

I was straight-up with my peeps. We had a competitor and we had to be ready. Since I didn't want to leave anything important on an answering machine, I called each one until I talked to them. I didn't go see them face-to-face. I wasn't gonna make Darkman's job any easier by leading him to my peeps.

Just when I was about to call Sonny to see if he set up a meeting with our suppliers, my cell rang.

"Yo."

"Ty, it's Alyse. I'm calling from school. Where are you?"

"At home. I ain't feeling well. Got a bad headache."

"Oh, no. I hope it goes away soon. Look, you should get a doctor's note. If you don't, they'll say you were cutting and—"

"Chill. I'll get a doctor's note tomorrow."

"Good. I don't want to see you get kicked out over this. They're mad strict around here."

"Yeah, I know. Thanks for the advice."

"I'll let you go. You should get some rest."

"I will. Holler at you later."

"Okay. Bye."

Click.

Man, I wished I could talk to her about Darkman. It felt wack, lying to Alyse. But there was no way I could tell her my business, because there was no way she'd back me up.

My work was just getting started. I stopped by a few choice spots: pool halls, take-outs, barbershops, delis, bars—all places where they knew me. Places where new faces would get noticed. Places where I could ask questions and get the straight-up goods.

I learned enough about my enemy to start a profile of him on my Palm Pilot.

Darkman:
- late twenties
- first name Kevin
- cocky
- Miami Crip connection
- family is big in Miami drug scene
- brought three guys with him from Florida (two black, one Hispanic, probably Cuban)
- has a high-maintenance girlfriend named Leanne

The question bugging me the most was why he was here in the first place. If he was so big in Miami, why did he leave?

Maybe the stories about him being a Florida big shot were made up. Or maybe his family was running the show and he decided to go off on his own. Maybe he came to Brooklyn because he had something to prove.

One thing was for sure: If Darkman thought he could just come to BK and crown himself a kingpin, he was wrong.

I was thinking of all this when I walked through the door

at 11:30 that night. Mom wasn't home, lucky for me. I needed to be alone to do some serious planning.

There was a postcard on the kitchen table.

Hey Ty,
How about them Giants? What a great game last night!
I'm missing your letters. Don't forget to write when you get
time.
Your dad

Anything about a sports team was our emergency code. Dad wanted me there ASAP.

ORLANDO'S SOLUTION

"WHAT I GOTTA SAY COULDN'T BE SAID OVER NO PHONE." JUST like my dad to get right to the point. "Word is, Kevin King's tryna take over. Calls himself Darkman."

"How'd you know?"

"Ain't no secret. I know the family. They too ambitious for they own good."

"Why the hell did he come to Brooklyn?"

"A few years back, his brother Max tried to run me outta business. Thought because I wasn't backed by a gang that he could set up shop right on top of me. He was wrong."

"What you do?"

"Brought him in. Fucked him up till he was almost dead. Sent him back to Miami."

"*Shit.* So this is Max's revenge?"

"I don't think this was Max's idea. He knows it would be setting up his brother for certain death. Nah, this is about Kevin wanting to show up his brothers. Kevin thinks if he can take over the Johnson territory—something Max couldn't do—he'll be on top."

"Do they know you're still in the picture?"

"Trust me, son, they know."

"You don't have to worry, Dad. We ain't giving up nothing to them. The situation is under control."

"No, it ain't. Not as long as Kevin King's around." Taking a folded piece of paper from his pocket, he passed it under the table. I slipped it into my pocket.

"What's this?"

"A phone number. Guy named Ronnie. He'll take care of King for us."

I swallowed. I never dealt with shit this heavy before.

"What if this guy fucks it up?"

"He won't. Ronnie's a professional. He know how to get the job done. No mistakes, no messes."

"This guy botches the job, and everybody points at me and Sonny."

"That's why I want you to use Ronnie and not some street thug. I used him a few times, and he always came through."

A *few times.*

"He ain't cheap, though, Ty. Professionals are never cheap. I probably paid him ten grand for the last one, and that was years back."

"Ten grand? You kidding me?"

"Probably more, with inflation."

"I ain't spending one red cent on that nigga King."

"You'll spend whatever you got to. Shit, you got cash coming out your ass, boy! Don't go cheap on something this important. Getting rid of King is an investment."

"A'ight, so I get rid of Kevin King, and the rest of his family wants revenge on my ass. Then what do I do? Hire Ronnie to eighty-six all of 'em?"

"Ty, I don't think you get what I'm telling you here. You got no choice but to get rid of him. You a man now, and you gotta act like one. You let him live, and it's *your* funeral. Sonny's, too."

"I ain't scared of him."

"If you ain't scared, then you too stupid to be running the family business."

"I'm holding shit down, Dad. I already got a plan to deal with him."

"'Course you do. You always been the man with the plan.

But I know how shit like this go down, and a man in your position gotta do whatever it takes to stay on top."

"I will, Dad. If I need Ronnie, I'll call him."

"Good." He smiled his dangerous smile. "'Cause if you won't, I will."

SCHOOL DAZE

I ROLLED OUT OF BED, SHOWERED, AND THREW SOME CLOTHES on, then went to the clinic up the block.

I had to wait an hour and a half in a waiting room full of screaming kids and wrinkly old people. By the time I got in to see the doctor, I really did have a headache.

The doctor was a middle-aged Chinese lady. I gave her a story about my horrible, skull-splitting headaches. She gave me a prescription for codeine and a note excusing my school absences. I wondered if I should fill the prescription and make a few bucks.

By ten o'clock I was going through the school metal detectors.

Rosie the security guard asked me, "Where *you* been?"

"Sick." I waved my doctor's note.

"Sick. Mmm-hmm. Get your scrawny ass to class."

"You say 'scrawny,' Rosie? Then you ain't seen this ass."

"And I don't want to." She waved me on.

I knew she wanted me.

After giving the doctor's note to the main office, I went to Math class, paid attention for three minutes, and then zoned out with my eyes half open.

The bell rang, jolting me awake.

I was hungry, for food and Alyse. I found her in the lunchroom lineup, asking the cafeteria lady to drain the oil off her spinach. When I came up beside her and whispered, "Hey, sugar," she jumped, almost dropping her tray.

"Ty! How are you feeling?"

"Good. I missed you, shorty."

I didn't realize it until now, but it was true. It had to be, because seeing her again felt damn good.

"Is your headache gone?"

"Yeah, but it'll come back if I don't get some eats. What've we got today?"

She made a face. "Hockey puck hamburgers, cardboard buns, cough-syrup grape drink."

"Oily spinach?"

"That too."

I snagged an orange tray, saying to the homies behind us, "It's okay, right?" They were smart enough not to say nothing, so I got in line behind her.

We paid with our lunch vouchers and sat down. Alyse took a few bites, then said, "I'm glad you're feeling better. My aunt used to get terrible headaches too. She'd shut herself up in her room and put the blinds down, sometimes for days at a time. Was yours like that?"

"Maybe not *that* bad. I just stayed in bed or on the couch, listened to some music, and relaxed."

"You can listen to music when you have a headache? What do you listen to?"

"A lot of different shit. K-Ron, Kanye West, G-Unit. Some old 'Pac. It don't bother my head if it ain't too loud."

"Have you heard that new K-Ron track, 'Livin' Large'? It's hot. But most of his stuff's just disgusting. Like the name of his album."

"Which one?"

"You know."

"Oh, you mean *Eatin' Out?*"

She nodded, too embarrassed to look at me.

"Tell me what you think of K-Ron," I said. "You think he's good-looking?"

"Yeah, he's cute. Do you think he's cute?"

"Me? I don't think any guy's cute. But that nigga's short, that's for sure. Five five if he's lucky. They make him look mad tall on TV."

"C'mon, he can't be that short."

"Five six, tops. I'm way taller than him."

"Have you seen him in person?"

"Seen him? He my homeboy."

"Yeah, right!"

"It's true."

She smacked my arm. "You're dreaming!"

"Think, Alyse. He's from Flatbush, don't you know? We been tight for years. Whenever he's in town, he calls me and we go out."

"Oh, yeah?"

"I usually meet him and his crew at a club."

"Like what club?"

"These days, that new one, the Wall."

"So you got fake I.D.?"

"Yeah. But I don't need it."

"Sure. What happens at the club? He got girls falling all over him?"

"Hell, yeah. But he stays in the VIP section most of the

time, so the honeys in his entourage are the only ones who can get close to him."

"I read in the *Post* that he's boozing and doing drugs every night. That true?"

"Uh-huh." Man, did I know it.

"I read he went to rehab last year."

"Stayed a week. Got bored."

"You tell a good story, Ty Johnson."

"I got the pictures to prove it. You'll see."

Being back at school wasn't so wack after all. Sitting in class, chilling with homies, playing some ball in the gym—it was all a break from the drama of the last couple of days.

After school, me and Alyse took the bus to the subway station.

Sonny was sitting in his Caddy waiting for me, music pumping.

He got out and gave Alyse a once-over. "Who this?"

Alyse stiffened. "Who *you*?"

Sonny burst out laughing.

"Sonny, Alyse. Alyse, Sonny."

"Ty's my partner in crime." Sonny nudged me. "Ain't that right?"

"Word." I said to Alyse, "I'll call you tonight, okay?"

"Okay." She looked a bit confused at my fast good-bye, but I'd say sorry later. I wished I could offer her a ride, but every second Sonny was around her was like a ticking time bomb.

Sonny and me got in the car.

"Be more fucking careful next time," I said.

"Huh? What I do?"

"The way you looked at her, for a start."

"She cute, that's all."

"Not every chick likes to be looked at that way."

Sonny raised his eyebrows. "I get it. You haven't balled her yet. You wanna make a good impression."

"Something like that. And she don't know I'm a hustler, so you got no business running your mouth like that. 'Partner in crime,' my ass!"

"Wait wait wait, hold up. She don't know what you do? C'mon, man, it'll help you ball her!"

"Not this girl. Enough of this, Sonny. Why you waiting for me?"

"I wanted to tell you we got a meeting tonight with Jones and Menendez."

"Good. You could've just called."

"Yeah, but I thought we should talk about your visit with Orlando before we see them. You told him about Darkman?"

"He already knew. Drive, I'll tell you everything."

But I didn't tell him everything.

SUPPLY AND DEMAND

THE GOVERNMENT LETS PEOPLE BUY JUNK FOOD THAT'S gonna rot their teeth and make them fat. The government lets people buy booze and cigarettes—both can kill you. But when it comes to drugs, the government don't trust the public to choose for themselves.

That forced hustlers like me and Sonny to go underground. Even though we had the dough to rent an office, Sonny and me had to meet suppliers and customers in secret places.

That night we were meeting Jones and Menendez. We'd used this place—an empty warehouse under the Manhattan Bridge—a few times before. When we pulled around the back of the warehouse, Sonny's high-beams lit up Menendez's dark blue Jag. Jones and Menendez had a thing about getting there first.

As we got out into the dark parking lot, Sonny said, "Hope they ain't freaked by the short notice." He switched on his flashlight.

Sonny had the jitter in his voice that he always had at night meetings. As for me, I liked the dark. It could be dangerous, but it could also be protection.

We went in through a side door and saw Jones and Menendez. From the looks of the place, it was being renovated. Scaffolding was up, and paint cans and two-by-fours were piled everywhere. This would have to be the last time we met here.

We went up to them and knocked knuckles. Menendez was a fat Dominican with an acne-scarred face and a thin mouth that didn't smile much. Jones wore a wife-beater under his leather jacket to show off his tattoos. Jones and Menendez grew up in the same project in Queens, and after a few years of competition hooked up as partners. Now, twenty years later, they was kingpins, living in Long Island mansions.

"Thanks for going outta your way," I said. "We got us some trouble. Figured you should get the heads-up."

They looked at each other, and Menendez said, "Go on."

"Some guy, calls himself Darkman, is trying to take over our business," Sonny explained.

I added quick, "We got no holes in our team. Our employees and customers are loyal, so that ain't a problem. But Darkman will try to find out who's supplying us."

"Will your employees tell him?" Jones asked.

Trick question. "*None* of our employees know who you are. Darkman won't find out shit from them. But Darkman was in the business down in Miami, and I know you said your Colombian friends land their planes near there."

"The Colombians is always talking to each other." Menendez gritted his teeth. "So if this muthafucka Darkman find out who we are, what he gonna do?"

Sonny answered, "Probably nothing. But there's a chance he might wanna cut a deal with you—bribe you into cutting off our supply."

"Tough shit for him," Jones said. "We don't play games. We'll tell him we ain't changing buyers."

"Good," I said. "If he contacts you, let me know."

Menendez's laugh was like a dog's bark. "We got ways of dealing with troublemakers. You just make sure you hang on to your customers."

"Our customers ain't going nowhere," Sonny promised.

Jones looked at me. "Why aren't you just having him knocked off?"

I didn't miss a beat. "We might have to, but I was upstate with my dad yesterday, and he was telling me about Darkman's family. They big and they got money. We don't need them wanting revenge. Plus, Dad's worried that if we knock him off, the cops'll start asking questions on the street."

Jones and Menendez nodded. These guys loved my dad. To them, his words were gospel.

We talked about the next shipment, then finished the meeting. Just as they wanted to be the first to get there, they liked to be the first to leave. We all slapped hands, and they headed out.

Jones stopped in the doorway of the warehouse. "Thanks for keeping us informed, fellas. You watch your backs, y'hear?"

I nodded. "We will."

JOB BENEFITS

"WHAT WAS UP WITH THAT GUY YESTERDAY?" ALYSE ASKED ME the next morning before Global History class. "He was shady."

"You in the habit of judging people you don't know?"

"It isn't like that. He just wasn't the type of guy I expected you to hang around with. You gotta admit, he's got the pimp thing going."

I laughed. "Sonny tries. He ain't no pimp. His girlfriend would have his balls in a sling."

"Good for her. By the way, guess who's in town?" She did a drumroll on the desk.

"The circus?"

"No, K-Ron! He's doing two shows and making a video."

"I know. Hey, I brought the pictures."

"You playing?"

"What, you didn't believe me?" I took a Kodak envelope from my book bag and gave it to her.

Alyse took the pictures from the envelope and flipped through them, her eyes wide. She saw pictures of K-Ron and me at clubs, restaurants, and backstage at a couple of concerts. She was grinning like a fool. She looked through them twice before giving them back.

"Those pictures are hot! I can't believe you're friends with K-Ron! Are you going to one of his shows while he's in town?"

I shrugged. "I dunno. I seen his shows so many times."

"Well, are you gonna meet up with him?"

"Sure, we'll chill."

"Wow. That's *whassup!*"

"I know what you thinking," I said. "You ain't getting within ten feet of K-Ron. Sure, he my homeboy, but he messed up. He'd be tryna wrap his sweaty body around you." I shook my head. "You too cute to put in the same room with K-Ron."

She laughed. "You're sweet."

"No, *you* sweet. That's why you ain't getting near K-Ron."

"The thing is, though . . . oh, forget it. It's not important."

"What is it?"

"Well . . ." She made a face. "I was just thinking, if I get him to autograph a few shirts, maybe I could make a little money. You know, sell them on eBay. You get something autographed, the price goes way up."

I pretended to look hurt. "You using me and K-Ron to get paid?"

"No! I didn't mean it that way!"

"Talk to the hand. I'm hurt. I'm hurting deep inside." I turned away from her. Then we both burst out laughing.

Mr. Guzman came into the classroom. "Looks like some of us are awake this morning!"

We said hi, and I turned back to Alyse. "Next time I see K-Ron, I'll get him to autograph some shirts for you."

"You wouldn't mind?"

"'Course not. It'll be cool to see how much you can sell 'em for."

"We'll split the profits fifty-fifty."

"No, thank you. Make me dinner sometime and we'll call it even."

She grinned. "Got yourself a deal."

• • •

At lunchtime I speed-dialed K-Ron from the boys' bathroom. It was 12:45, around the time he usually woke up.

"K-Ron, what up?"

His voice was all scratchy. "I woke up with two hot bitches in my bed. But *damn* I got a muthafucka of a hangover."

"Big night last night?"

"Every night, homey. Every night."

"You must've run outta stuff by now, huh? How about I drop by tonight?"

"Huh? Sorry, these hos is distracting me. I'll pass on the shit for now. My manager's threatening to throw my black ass back into rehab if I show up at the studio high again. Says Jason Jay won't work with me no more if I don't clean up."

"That's heavy, man."

"Damn straight. Anyway, I'm gonna stick to booze and smokes for the next little while. When I go back on the road I can wild out."

"A'ight. Gimme a call before you leave and I'll hook you up."

"You got it."

"And K-Ron, do me a favor? Send me a few autographed shirts for my girls?"

"I'll tell my assistant."

"Good stuff. Peace out, playa."

"Peace."

SECRET INTELLIGENCE
REPORT 001

THAT AFTERNOON I GOT A PHONE MESSAGE FROM MONFREY.

"Ty, I got a report. Meet me at Thai Take-Out at five."

Thai Take-Out was on Bedford Avenue, in Williamsburg. I found Monfrey at the counter, ordering food. Even though his back was to me, he didn't jump when I put a hand on his shoulder.

"What up, Ty?"

"Hey, Monfrey. What you order?"

"Number six."

"I'll take the same," I told the Asian guy behind the counter. I paid for both, and Monfrey said thanks.

We got our food, then sat down at one of the four small tables. The only other people in the place were two white ladies, one with a baby in a stroller beside her.

Monfrey sat across from me, his hygiene no worse, but no better, than usual. He wore an old red Adidas sweat suit. Some might call it retro, but on Monfrey it looked old and out of style. At least the comb that stood straight up in his Afro matched his gear. Too bad his blue kicks threw the whole thing off.

Monfrey got right to the point. "I'm in."

"And?"

"They got me running so many errands, they calling me Gopher. One of them came up to me in the park and offered me weed. I told him I'd do some running for them if they'd gimme some. Kevin got me making little deliveries, grabbing them pizza and shit."

"Kevin. Anybody call him Darkman?"

"He calls himself that. He's a regular guy who thinks he ain't a regular guy." Monfrey talked with food in his mouth, so his words came out garbled. "He thinks it's his destiny to take over your territory. He talks about you a lot. Knows about Sonny, too. But he says it's you, not Sonny, who's in charge."

"What else does he say about me?" I forked noodles into my mouth.

"That you too young and inexperienced to handle him, and

that you'll be done by the end of the year, one way or the other."

"I don't like the sound of that. Is he planning something?"

"Don't know."

I chewed my noodles slow. "Tell me about his crew."

"He got three guys with him from Miami. Crow, Natty, and Alejandro. The three of 'em live together just a few blocks from him and Leanne in Bed-Stuy. Kevin and Crow is tight—Crow got some say in how shit goes down. The others, you know, just do what Kevin tells them."

"What do they do for him?"

"They find new customers. They sell on the street."

"They use?"

"C'mon now, Ty. We *all* use." He grinned like a fool.

My eyes narrowed. "You keep it under control."

"I will."

"Do you know who messed up Carlos?"

"All of 'em, and they had fun doing it. Especially Alejandro. He's one sick bitch." His mouth twisted like he tasted something sour.

"These fellas loyal to their boss?"

"I guess so. They all been working for the family since they was young."

"So they happy with him? No complaints?"

"Oh, they be complaining. They barely getting paid because Darkman ain't bringing in much cash."

"Work on getting them to trust you. Especially Crow."

"I been working on it. The dumber he thinks I am, the more he'll say around me. Gimme a couple weeks."

TURKEY SHOOT

OVER THE LOUDSPEAKER THE NEXT DAY, THE STUDENT announcer said, "Get ready, Les Chancellor High! Today is our annual turkey shoot!"

The class cheered. "Does this mean we get outta class?" I asked the guy behind me.

"You got it. *Everybody* does the turkey shoot, 'cause once you out, you get to stay and watch. Nobody goes back to class all day."

At 10 a.m. we got out of class. The dividing wall between the boys' and girls' gyms was taken down so we could watch the whole competition. Everybody went to their assigned baskets. I lined up with the guys at Hoop 6.

Scanning the gym for Alyse, I spotted her at Hoop 12, stretching on the floor with a few other girls. I looked around at my competition, thinking it would be cool if I could win this thing. I always was a solid shooter. When I got into the zone, I never missed.

I grabbed a ball from one of the bins and started dribbling, bouncing it on my knee, then under my leg, testing my concentration.

My first practice shot was a *swish*. Nothing but net.

A whistle got everybody's attention. The competition was starting.

Coach Hayes was in charge of Hoop 6. "All right, guys, line up over here. I'll call your names one by one. You have ten seconds to shoot. Remember, you step over the free-throw line and your shot's invalid. No re-shots allowed." He looked down at his clipboard. "First up, Inman, Elijah."

Elijah did a little fancy bouncing, then released the ball. I knew right away that its arc was all wrong. It clanked off the rim.

With his head hanging low, he went to stand with the other eliminated guys on the far wall.

The next shooter did better, but the one after that wasn't so lucky.

It was my turn. Taking position, I bounced the ball once, twice, three times, getting into the zone. I looked up, rose up, *swish*!

A beauty.

Half an hour later, I was the last man standing in my group. Ryan Bailey gave me a run for my money, but in the end, his shot bounced off the rim.

Before lining up with the other male finalists at Hoop 1, I went to the fountain for a long drink. When I looked up, Alyse was standing there.

"You're doing great," she said. "Everyone's been saying you got fine form."

"Thanks. How'd you do?"

She laughed. "I didn't even make the first basket. The ball didn't get anywhere near it!"

I couldn't help laughing too. "I'm glad you can laugh at yourself."

"Why not? I know my strengths. Basketball's not one of them. But at least I can miss a day of classes. Not that I would've minded those Knicks tickets."

"*Knicks* tickets?"

"Well, it isn't official, but the president of the Student Council told me last week that she was trying to get two pairs of tickets for the guy and girl winners."

"That's banging. If I win, I know who I'll bring."

Her eyes lit up.

The whistle blew. "I better get back."

She kissed my cheek. "I'll be cheering for you."

I walked across the gym and lined up with the finalists. I slapped the hand of the homeboy in front of me, a white guy called Austen Forrester. He was a ball player with mad skills.

One by one, the guys took their shots. I landed mine with no problems.

So did the others.

Each guy had his own technique. Some jumped clear off the floor as they shot, others went on tiptoe. Some dribbled before shooting, others stood, ball-in-hand, staring directly at the net. Some did tricks for the crowd, others paid the crowd no mind, and tried to get into the zone.

My second shot was clean. Cheers broke out from the stands. I looked over my shoulder to see Alyse jumping up and down. I blew her a kiss, making the crowd wild out.

I took my place in line again, dribbling to get back my focus. The crowd let out a huge "Awwww" as Drew McDermott's shot spun around the rim, almost dipped in, but instead spun out. A heartbreaker.

Soon there was only six of us. We went three rounds that way.

Then five. Henry's ball bounced out off the backboard.

Then four. George's shot didn't have enough spin.

Then three. Dayate let out a howl as the net coughed up his ball.

The two finalists were me and Austen Forrester. His shots were as perfect as mine.

So how could I beat him?

What would Sun Tzu say?

When you're up against a force of equal power, the answer isn't to try to prove you're better. The answer is to wait for an advantage.

I didn't need to sweat about beating Austen Forrester, I realized. I only had to keep up *my* game. Eventually he would make a mistake.

Before Austen could take the next shot, a whistle blew. My head shot up. The president of the Student Council, Martina Léon, walked up to us with a microphone. "Before you take your final shots, I want to announce what the winner's prize will be."

The crowd booed the interruption.

"Shhh . . . Look, believe me, this prize is worth knowing about, and I'm sure it'll motivate these guys even more. The prize is two Knicks tickets! And not just any Knicks tickets. They're fifth row!"

The crowd cheered.

"Les Chancellor High would like to thank the Knicks' Tickets for Achievers program for donating the tickets. Let's give it up for the Knicks and our finalists!"

I groaned, bouncing the ball over and over, pissed off at the interruption. I looked at Austen, whose eyes were bugging out. He wanted those tickets bad. Would it throw him off?

"Shhh . . . Quiet, everyone," Martina said. "Let's get back to the competition." She walked to the side, and the whistle blew again.

Austen stepped up, shot, scored.

I walked up, shot, scored.

Austen scored again.

I scored again.

He scored again.

I scored again. Austen cursed and stamped his foot.

My eyes were glued to the ball as Austen released his next shot. It hit the front of the rim and bounced out.

The crowd booed and cheered.

To win, I had to land this shot.

I walked up to the line, trying to tune out the hoopla in the stands, trying not to picture Alyse and the rest of the school watching me.

In my mind, I was thirteen again. It was after dark, and I was the only kid left on the court. I been trying for ages to land ten in a row, and I was gonna stay as long as it took. Sure, Dad was locked up. But when I got drafted to the NBA, he'd be able to watch me on TV. I'd landed nine shots so far. . . .

I dribbled several times, tattooing the line at my toes. After I positioned the ball just right with the NBA label showing on top, I took my jump and let it fly.

Swish!!!

The net hugged the ball for a second before dropping it to the floor.

People from the stands rushed onto the courts, surrounding me. Alyse ran up, and I caught her in a big hug.

"Ty, that was so amazing!"

"*You're* amazing, boo."

I felt a tap on my shoulder. It was Martina. "Congratulations! Here are the tickets!"

I looked down at Alyse. "So, wanna go to a Knicks game?"

When something sounds too good to be true, it usually is.

Sitting beside Alyse in the bleachers watching the girls' final, I realized I couldn't take her to the Knicks game. It wasn't safe to be out in public with her, especially in fifth-row seats at an NBA game.

Maybe the chance that Darkman would go after Alyse was small, but *any* chance was too much. Alyse wouldn't want to be a part of this game.

I shouldn't be with her at all.

I looked at her, something tightening in my chest. It was too late.

I tapped her leg with the tickets. "Alyse, I better give you these."

"Scared you might lose them?"

"Yeah, or somebody might jump me for them after school."

She laughed and tucked them into her bag. "I'll keep them safe." Turning her attention back to the game, she got up and cheered when her friend landed a basket. "Goooo, Kristen!"

I figured I'd call her at the last minute and cancel. Alyse could call up a friend, or even take her mom. It was all good.

I reached over and took her hand, giving it a squeeze. She smiled at me. We didn't need words.

Yeah, it was all good.

FAMILY MATTERS

FAMILY PARTIES WERE WACK. ON THE JOHNSON SIDE, YOU HAD a bunch of crackheads, like my late uncle Jean. I used to sit next to him on the couch while he talked shit, guzzled cheap wine, and went to the bathroom for hits.

On the Greaves side, you had a bunch of saps. Mom had four sisters, who all had babies by pricks and players. Family get-togethers had lots of tears, bitching about men, greasy soul food, more tears, wine, and more bitching about men.

So when, over the phone, Alyse asked me to come to her mom's Halloween party, I made up an excuse.

"Wish I could, but I gotta work. I probably won't get off till late."

"Oh, that's too bad. But I understand."

I don't think Alyse was trying to make me feel guilty, but

I did. A few minutes later I called her back. "Just talked to my boss. He's gonna let me go early."

"You're so sweet!"

But when the night came, I was feeling sour. I spent that whole rainy Saturday making deliveries, and I was wiped. But I couldn't back out. Alyse was waiting for me, and I didn't want to let her down.

At least I didn't have to wear no Halloween costume. After showering, I put on black pants and a white sweater from Banana Republic, with shiny black shoes. Preppy clothes made my white customers feel comfortable, so I had lots of them. They didn't want their dealer showing up in Enyce or Sean John. Those brands had ghetto written all over them.

I walked past Mom, who was on the couch watching TV and eating Cheez Doodles. I threw on my jacket and was reaching for the doorknob when she asked, "Where ya off to, honey?"

"A friend's Halloween party."

"Which friend?"

"Janelle." I never told her the names of people I hung out with.

"Janelle, hmm?"

"It ain't like that, Ma. She and a bunch of homies from school will be there."

"Oh, that's so nice!" She got off the couch and walked up to me, straightening the collar of my jacket. I gritted my teeth, hoping Cheez Doodle dust wasn't messing it up.

Guess she was in one of her *mama* moods. It was annoying when she got this way. But her *naggy mama* moods were worse.

"I'm so happy you doing well at school and you made lots of friends. It ain't easy starting over somewhere else, but you done great. Everyone always took to you, Ty, ever since you was a little boy. Even your teachers!"

"Can't blame them."

"For a while I was afraid your father was influencing you too much."

Five seconds to bitchy mama. Four, three, two . . .

But she just shook her head. "Anyway, I'm real glad you invited to a party. What arc you bringing?"

"Bringing?" *Shit*, I didn't even think of getting a gift.

"You can't go to a party without bringing something." She tapped my lapel. "Now you wait here. I don't want people thinking my son is cheap."

She hurried down the hallway in her fluffy pink slippers, stuck her head in a closet, and came out with a box of chocolates.

"Don't it look expensive? I won it in a raffle at work. I was gonna save it for the holidays."

"It's perfect, Mom." I reached for my wallet.

"Put that away now. Just take it and get yourself to the party. I bet you already late. Go on."

"Mom, thanks."

She smiled. "Night, honey. Go on now."

Half an hour later, Alyse welcomed me with a hug.

"I'm so glad you came, Ty!"

"Me too, shorty."

She backed out of my arms, giggling. "Look at you, all clean-cut and preppy."

"You like?"

"Uh-huh. You got class written all over you, son."

"So do you, boo."

Our eyes locked. No doubt about it, we were feeling each other.

A bump against my leg broke the moment. It was Gavin, dressed as Batman in a purple suit and cape.

Alyse picked him up. "He's supposed to be playing in the bedroom with his cousins. I bet he heard your voice and ran out to see if it was you."

"Hey, Gavin. How you doing, Little G?" I tickled the top of his head.

A lady wearing black clothes and a cat mask came up to us. "Is this Ty, dear?"

"Mom, the mask . . ."

She took off her mask. Alyse's mom had a strong handshake and a Phylicia Rashad smile. "So nice to finally meet you, Ty."

I gave her the chocolates. "Thanks for having me, Ms. —"

"Call me Yvonne."

"Pleased to meet you."

She grinned and tapped Alyse's shoulder. "I like this boy. Make yourself at home, Ty. There's plenty of food. Enjoy yourself." She went off toward the kitchen.

Alyse bounced Gavin in her arms. "Let's take him back to the bedroom. Cousin Sarah's reading scary stories. Then I'll introduce you to the rest of my family."

"You the boss, honey."

She winked at me. "You figured that out quick."

Over the next hour, I also figured out that her family wasn't half bad. Halloween at home was a family tradition since nobody wanted to take the kids trick-or-treating in a neighborhood with a rep for Halloween eggings, muggings, and drive-bys. There must've been six or seven little kids running around the place. I tried not to step on any of them.

The whole apartment was done up with plastic spiderwebs, black and orange streamers, and colored lightbulbs. In the living room, space was cleared for a dance floor. Alyse's bedroom was Candy Central. I spent some time chilling there with the kids, and even swapped my Mars bar for a Twix with her six-year-old cousin Vicky.

All and all, her family seemed like good people. But I had to stop myself from laughing when Aunt Grace asked, "What church do you go to?"

"I'm Presbyterian," I answered. "My mom's a church elder."

"Is she? She's setting a good example for you."

"Definitely."

Alyse came up beside me. "He's from a good family," she said.

Good thing she don't know about Orlando.

Aunt Grace said, "This family's AME, but we like Presbyterians, too." She winked and walked away.

Alyse nudged me. "So you're a Presbyterian, are you?"

"You got it."

She put a hand on her hip. "When's the last time you went to church?"

"Um, let me think . . ."

She laughed.

A few minutes later, on a sugar high from Cousin Riqui's Halloween punch, I let Alyse drag me onto the dance floor with the kids. Michael Jackson's *Thriller* was playing. That album was the sound track of my childhood. I taught the kids some of the hot dance moves I had worked on over the years, especially my Moonwalk. Alyse cheered me on.

We collapsed onto the sofa, out of breath.

My cell phone rang. Sonny's number. "Yeah?"

"You want the bad news, or the motherfucking awful news?"

"What happened?"

"K-Ron got busted with a shitload of coke in his trunk."

"Whoa." I closed my eyes. "That ain't good."

"Guess who he fingered as his dealers?"

"Who?"

"Us. You and me."

"Don't play me."

"I ain't playing you, Ty."

"I'm on my way over."

"Wait! Should I pack a bag and get outta here? I mean, do you think the cops are gonna pick me up?"

"Just stay put. I'll be there in a few minutes." I hung up.

"What's going on?" Alyse looked worried.

"A friend's in trouble. Sorry, but I gotta bounce. I better go say good-bye to your family." I got up. "I'll call you tomorrow about the Knicks game. I'm thinking we'll meet around six."

"Okay." She got up and touched my face. "Seriously, Ty, is there something I can do? Can I come with you?"

"It wouldn't be a good idea." I kissed her cheek. "But thanks, Alyse. Tonight's been great."

But I knew the night wasn't gonna stay that way.

A BLADE IN THE BACK

WITHIN TEN MINUTES I WAS IN A CAB, COACHING SONNY OVER my cell phone. "You got nothing to worry about, Sonny. The stuff wasn't from us. We been set up."

"Set up? But we the ones supplying K-Ron!"

"Chill, a'ight? Have a beer. I'll be there in ten." I snapped the phone shut.

I wanted to smash my fist into the seat. Smash it like I was hitting K-Ron's and Darkman's faces. But Ty Johnson didn't lose control.

Taking a few breaths, I leaned back into the seat.

A few minutes later I gave the driver a twenty and walked into Sonny's building, real calm in case somebody was watching. Sonny buzzed me up. As soon as I was in the hallway in front of his apartment, he swung the door open and I went inside.

I saw that Sonny had an overstuffed gym bag at the door.

"You said the coke ain't from us, right?" Sonny was mad panicked.

"Right. We gotta unpack that bag right away. The cops could come anytime to search your place. If it looks like you running, it looks like you done something wrong. Come on." I grabbed the bag, and we went into the bedroom. "Where's Desarae?"

"At her mom's in Queens."

"Good."

We started unpacking.

I said, "When I heard K-Ron was back in town last week, I gave him a call. It was weird. Usually K-Ron calls me the same night he gets in town. He didn't this time. I only heard he was in town because my"—*damn, I almost said girlfriend*—"because my homey read it in the *Post*. When I called, he said he didn't need anything this time. Said his manager was gonna put him in rehab again if he didn't slow down. Looks like K-Ron got another supplier. It's gotta be Darkman."

Sonny looked up from his gym bag. "You think Darkman set K-Ron up as a way to bring us down?"

"I don't know. Maybe K-Ron got caught, and Darkman saw a chance to bring us down by telling K-Ron to sell us out."

"Why would K-Ron do that? I thought you two was tight."

"I bet Darkman got plenty of ways to be convincing."

"Do you think the cops are gonna come after us?"

"'Course they will, but they won't be able to prove shit." I looked him dead in the eye. "Now promise me you ain't got an ounce of nothing in here."

"I don't keep nothing big here, you know that. I ain't suicidal. But I got a tiny bit of weed and a pipe."

"A milligram is too much if they come sniffing. Let's get rid of it."

He went to the nightstand, took out a small bag of weed and a bong from the drawer. In the bathroom, Sonny poured the weed into the toilet and cut the bag into pieces, then flushed. I smashed the glass bong against the counter, then crushed the pieces under my feet, scooped it up with my bare hands, and flushed it a few pieces at a time.

"Anything else in here, Sonny? Think."

"Nothing." He was breathing hard. "They don't have anything on us, do they, Ty? They can't touch us."

"Right. Remember that when they questioning you. We friends. You don't know K-Ron from any other nigga. They can place *me* with him, not you. You got nothing to worry about."

"So what you gonna say?"

I came up with the story in the cab. "Me and K-Ron used to be friends, but we ain't anymore because he accused me of being jealous and talking trash about him. He hates me now, and that's why he fingered me as his dealer."

"I got you."

"When the cops follow up a lead on us and it turns up cold, it'll be done. Sure, they'll know we ain't choir boys—they already know that—but it won't be enough."

Sonny nodded, taking it all in. Sweat dripped off his face. "I trust you, Ty. You won't sell me out."

"Selling you out would be selling *myself* out."

"I know. It's just, this Darkman's making me crazy."

"That's what he wants. He's hoping the po-po will find something on us or our names will get leaked to the papers. His plan won't work. We unshakable. Did I ever let you down, Sonny?"

He shook his head. "No, nigga."

"Then why would I do it now? In this business, we brothas. Remember that."

Suddenly the front door burst open and shouting filled the apartment.

I felt a body slam into me, shoving me to the ground. Heavy arms pulled my hands behind my back and smashed my face into the carpet.

Cuffs snapped around my wrists. Cops started searching the place, looking for drugs or cash. They wouldn't find either.

"I hope you got a warrant!" Sonny shouted.

"Wouldn't leave home without it, Mr. Blake," said one of the pigs. "Come on, we're taking you in."

They yanked us to our feet and took us down in the elevator, then hustled us into different cars. "Easy, I ain't struggling," I said.

On the way to the station, one of the cops said over his shoulder, "So, I hear you and K-Ron are buddies."

"Not anymore," I said.

"I guess he ruined the friendship when he ratted you out, huh?" He laughed. "K-Ron used to take you to some wild parties, I bet."

"I never been much of a partyer."

"You mean to tell me you don't like to party?"

I didn't say nothing.

"What's the matter, kid? You deaf or something?"

"I wish."

"What's that?"

"Nothing."

I didn't have to deal with his stupid questions for long because the precinct was nearby. As we pulled into the lot, I got ready for what was coming.

I knew a little something about interrogations. My dad went through enough of them. *If they bring ya in, don't sweat it. Stay cool and stick to yo' story.*

The cops took me inside the precinct. Nobody gave me a second look. A young black man coming in was nothing new to them.

This whole thing was messed up. The one time I *didn't* do the deal, they brought me in.

An officer led me into a gray room with paint peeling off the walls, and left me alone.

This was when I was supposed to sweat.

An hour later, I still wasn't sweating.

After the second hour, I still wasn't sweating, but I was damn bored, and pissed that they were wasting my time.

I closed my eyes and relived my night with Alyse.

When the door opened, the detective found me as calm as if I'd been lying on a beach in the Caribbean.

He was big and dark-skinned. If I was a skinny white guy, I might've been scared. Still, his black eyes grabbed my attention. "I'm Detective Akindele."

I cleared my throat. "Hey."

"Do you know why you're here?"

"No, sir."

"Do you know K-Ron Maxwell?"

"Yeah."

"Have you heard what happened to him?"

"He got arrested."

"Now do you know why you're here?"

As a character witness? I wanted to say. "Maybe you could tell me, Detective Akindele."

"Probable cause, Johnson. Do you know what that is?"

"It's when the police got reason to pick somebody up, question them, maybe search their place, but not charge them."

He seemed impressed. "Not bad at all. Did you study law in school?"

"Yes, sir." But law class wasn't where I learned about

probable cause. Most hustlers knew the words that told them if they were busted. It went something like this:

Probable cause: They ain't got shit on you.

Charged: We got evidence on your ass.

Probation: You one small step away from going up north, homeboy.

Community service: Here's another way to find new customers.

Akindele cut into my thoughts. "K-Ron had a few things to say about you. Can you guess what?"

"No, sir."

"Tell me, what was it your father did for a living?"

"He was a full-time hustler."

Akindele smiled. "That's one way of putting it. And why did he go to jail?"

"He was convicted of drug dealing. What does this have to do with K-Ron, Detective?"

"I was just trying to establish your understanding of the charges that could be filed against you."

This Akindele thought he was the shit.

It was gonna be a long night.

• • •

I didn't get home until eight o'clock the next morning. All I could think of was falling into bed and passing out.

I opened the door, blinked. "Fuck is this?" Cupboards emptied, drawers opened, sofa cushions on the floor, papers everywhere.

Mom burst into the front hall, dressed in her pink bathrobe and slippers. "Look, look at this place! Look what they did to it! Like it was no better than a crackhouse! What are the neighbors thinking with the cops searching my home?"

"Mom, I'm sorry. I'll clean this up. They tried to pin something on me, but I didn't do it. They won't be pressing charges."

She squeezed my arm, hard. "They told me you was running with Sonny, that no-good nigga."

"Mom—"

"What, you gonna deny it? Go ahead, then. Deny it."

"Sonny and me—"

"Go ahead. I'm waiting."

I hung my head.

"I wouldn't have been stupid enough to believe you, anyway." She wrenched her hand away. "You your daddy's child, ain't you?"

"Shut up."

"Don't you talk to me like that!"

I stalked past her, going to my room.

She followed me, standing in the doorway with her arms crossed. "You had it too good, you always did. I'm working my ass off to pay the bills while you be running the streets with Sonny! Well, no more, baby boy."

I lost it. "What—you kicking me out? Well, I'll make it easy for you." I grabbed a duffel bag and started shoving clothes in.

"You wanna leave, huh? See what it's like when you ain't got mama taking care of you all the time? Go ahead!"

"I'm gone." Grabbing the bag, I pushed past her and walked out. She slammed the door behind me.

The red numbers on the alarm clock said: 5:34. In the morning? At night? I rolled, feeling fat pillows around me. Where the hell was I?

My foggy mind figured it out. After the fight with Mom, I called a cab and went to a hotel. I'd rented rooms here before, sometimes with girls, but mostly to make deals. It was clean, comfortable, and the staff didn't ask questions.

I listened to my messages.

Sonny: 2:50 a.m. *"They grilled me, but they didn't get nothing. Damn pigs gave me forty-five minutes of their time, no more. Call me when you get out."*

Sonny: 3:32 a.m. *"They still got you there, Ty? What's going on? Call me ASAP. I'm gonna crash, but I got my phone on."*

Sonny: 10:12 a.m. *"Where you at, man? They still got you?"*

Sonny: 1:30 p.m. *"Ty, where the fuck are you? Get your ass on that phone."*

There were three more messages from Sonny. Then I heard Alyse's voice.

"Hey, just calling to talk about the plan tonight. I thought maybe we could meet at Madison Square Garden since Mom and Gavin and I are going shopping in the city. Call my cell."

"Ty, me again, call me about tonight."

The last one was left ten minutes ago. *"Ty, what's going on? I'm at Madison Square Garden already, I have the tickets. Are you coming?"*

Damn.

I called her cell phone, and the voice mail picked up. I was getting off easy. "Alyse, hi, it's me. Looks like I can't make it to the game. I'm mad sorry I didn't call before, but I got serious family stuff going on. You still got time to call a friend to go with you. Bye." I hung up, feeling like shit.

I dialed room service. "Burger and fries please. And a Caesar salad and Coke."

Then I called Sonny.

"Ty! I thought you was all shot up, lying in a ditch somewhere!"

"Don't be joking like that, Sonny."

"I ain't joking! Where the hell did you go?"

"I went to the Dunsmore and fell asleep. Got into a fight with Mom. Po-po trashed the crib. And they told her you and me is tight."

"Shit!"

"Tell me about it. Anyway, they kept me at the station all night. Grilled me. It ain't you they wanted, Sonny, it's me. Come over in an hour. We'll talk."

"Good. I'll tell Jones and Menendez to come too. They been bugging all day, but they didn't wanna meet without you there."

"Who'd you talk to?"

"Menendez."

"How'd he sound?"

"Worried. He heard we got picked up."

"Did he mention K-Ron?"

"No. But I bet they put it together."

"Tell him they can show up between eight and nine. Room 42. You be here at seven."

"A'ight."

I hung up and switched on CNN. Soon the headline crossed the bottom of the screen. *Rap star K-Ron charged with possession of narcotics.* I flicked to CBS-2, Fox 5, and UPN, and caught the tail end of a couple of reports about K-Ron. They had the same information: that cocaine was found in his trunk, and that the arraignment would be early next week.

Room service came quick, and I stuffed a tip into the guy's hand. I ate fast, stopping only for a few sips of Coke to make it go down smooth.

By the time Sonny showed up, I was showered and awake.

Sonny threw his coat over a chair. "The hell happened last night, son? I can't believe they kept you there all damn night!"

My cell rang. "One sec, Sonny. I gotta take this." I opened the phone. "Hey, Mom."

"Ty, sweetie, where you at? Come home, we need to talk. Have you eaten yet?"

"Chill, Mom. I ain't coming back just yet. Gimme a few days to think about things."

"You ain't at Sonny's, are you?"

"There you go again, Mom."

"I'm sorry, honey. I just—"

"Listen, I'll call you soon. I'm staying at a friend's and no, it ain't Sonny."

Sonny was watching me, smiling.

"Then who? Cheddar?"

"I'm not gonna tell you because I don't want you coming over. Don't worry, everything's cool. Talk to you soon."

"But—"

"Bye, Mom."

Sonny smacked his knee. "Poor Georgina! First Orlando, then you. I'm surprised she didn't murder you when she found out we was hanging together."

"I'm glad there was no gun around. Anyway, what was I saying? Oh, last night. They kept me waiting for two hours trying to make me sweat. Then this Detective Akindele grilled me like a steak, but I stayed rare. I wasn't gonna admit to picking my nose, much less hustling. They got nothing on me, so they had to let me go. Did you hear any more about K-Ron?"

"Just that he's being arraigned on Monday." He went to the minibar, unscrewed a little bottle, and swigged. "Guess you won't be there to give moral support, huh?"

I grunted.

DISHONOR AMONG THIEVES

JONES AND MENENDEZ SHOWED UP AT EIGHT. SONNY LET them in.

"We heard you fellas got picked up last night." Jones's jacket hung open, his muscles tight under his wife-beater. "Rumor has it K-Ron fingered you as his connection. We want to know if that's true."

Sonny said, "Sorry, man, but we don't name our customers."

I shot Sonny a look, letting him know I'd handle this. He wasn't sensing them like I was. "Yeah, we got picked up last night because K-Ron said we were his dealers. We supplied him in the past, but the stuff he was caught with wasn't from us."

"Then why'd he say so?" Menendez asked.

"Darkman must've been the one who supplied him," I said. "He's gotta be holding something big over K-Ron's head to get him to rat us out."

A vein popped out in Jones's neck. "What the cops got on *you*?"

"Jack shit," I said. "We'd still be locked up if they had anything on us. They won't be pressing charges, and we won't be needing no lawyer."

"So you saying Kevin King is behind this?" Menendez stared at us. "Why haven't you dusted him yet?"

I cleared my throat. "I'm taking care of it. You got nothing to worry about."

Jones scoffed. "We been worried ever since this guy reared his ugly-ass head. You got a game plan in case you get charged?"

"Hearsay ain't enough to charge us," I said. "But even if it happened, you wouldn't get sucked in. You know that, right?" I looked from one to the other.

They didn't say nothing, but Menendez took a brown envelope from his briefcase. "We brought this just to make sure."

I reached out to take the envelope, but he dropped it on the dresser instead. "No hurry. Have a look at it when we leave. And don't take it the wrong way, man. It's just—"

"Insurance," Jones finished for him.

My hands curled into fists. I wasn't gonna like what was in that envelope. "So, is this all you wanted to talk about?"

Menendez said, "Yeah. That's all. We gotta go. We still got business tonight."

They left fast. Sonny got to the envelope before I did. He tore it open. The first page was a picture of a girl getting into her car. The next was a closer picture of her. She didn't seem to know the camera was there.

"What the *fuck*?" Sonny roared.

"Who's the girl?" She looked kind of familiar.

"My sister."

The next picture was of my mom behind the cash register at her job. She smiled for the camera, probably thinking the person taking the picture was a tourist.

She didn't know the picture would be used to threaten her life.

Sonny smashed his hand on the table. "I'm'a snuff those motherfuckers for this!"

"We ain't gonna touch them, and they ain't gonna touch our families. They just warning us not to sell 'em out."

"After all these years, they don't trust us? And they pull this shit!"

"They bluffing. They know that if they touch our families Orlando will take 'em down. These pictures are telling us they in control."

"So what, we supposed to forget they threatened our peeps?"

"They don't want us to forget it. But they know we won't do nothing stupid."

"They fuck with my family, I get stupid."

"With Darkman around, we gotta play it cool. We don't need more enemies."

Sonny waved a picture in my face. "Ain't this telling us we enemies? Y'ever had a friend threaten your mama before?"

"Look, Sonny, they ain't the worst we gotta deal with right now. As soon as Darkman is out of the picture, we'll find new suppliers. For right now, it ain't smart to change."

"That's fucked up!" He went over to a chair and plunked down. "Where's Orlando when you need him?"

I didn't answer. My eyes were still on the pictures. The way I saw it, a bond was broken. It was a bond of trust that had lasted from the time they worked with my dad until now.

The messed-up part was, they didn't need to go and threaten us like that. We'd never sell them out. That was our code.

First K-Ron stabbed us in the back, now Jones and Menendez were threatening us. Maybe honor among thieves was bullshit.

I looked at Sonny. Would he sell me out if the price was right? If we both got charged one day, would he testify against me if it meant he could walk?

Could I blame him if he did? After all, if I got locked up I wouldn't have as hard a time as most brothers since I was Orlando Johnson's son. Sonny wouldn't get the same protection.

But Sonny wasn't my partner, hadn't been my dad's helper, because he was smart. He was with us because he was loyal.

That kind of loyalty was rare, especially in this business.

INNOCENCE

MONDAY MORNING I CAME TO SCHOOL HALFWAY THROUGH
Earth Science class. Alyse glanced back at me, frowned, and
looked away.

I could've used one of her sweet smiles this morning,
but I didn't blame her for being salty with me. I ran out on
her Friday night and ditched her Saturday—not that
Knicks tickets weren't a hot consolation. I had to think up
a good family emergency if she was ever gonna talk to me
again.

And then there was Mom, who kept leaving messages
telling me to come home. The more I thought about it, the
more I knew I should stay away for now. It's not just that Mom
would be constantly in my business. With all the Darkman
shit going on, it was safer for her if I stayed away.

Sonny kept asking me why I still bothered going to school. Fact was, I didn't know. Maybe I needed a break from the streets, or maybe it was to be around Alyse.

Hell, maybe it was because, for a few hours in the day, my life felt normal.

When class ended, I tried to catch Alyse, but Ms. Millons caught me first. Her blue eyes stared right through me. "Where were you? And before you answer, know that I intend to verify whatever you say."

"I slept in. It ain't an excuse, and I know that if it happens again I'll be sent to the dean."

I took the words right out of her mouth except, "You're doing well in this class, Ty. I think you have a seventy-five. But you know what? You have an aptitude in this field and you could be getting nineties."

"I like it."

"You're a very capable young man. You just have to decide how to use those capabilities."

"How about for Earth Science?"

"Good answer." She smiled, but her eyes didn't trust me. I didn't trust me either.

I left the class, stopping when I heard my name.

Alyse was waiting for me. She hugged her books to her

chest, looking so innocent. *Too innocent to be hanging out with me.*

"I know you must be mad about Saturday night," I said.

"Mad? Of course I'm not mad. I heard all about what happened. I know what you meant by 'family emergency.' Under the circumstances, I don't blame you."

I was blown away. "You know what happened?"

"It was all over the TV and the papers. Everyone's been following the K-Ron story."

"Wait, so you know . . ."

"Yeah, I know he was caught with drugs. It's so sad, isn't it?"

I nodded.

She shifted her books into her left arm and took my hand. "It must've been hard for you seeing that happen to your friend."

"Uh, yeah." It took me a second to figure out what she was talking about. "His family was pretty broken up. I spent most of the weekend with them."

"I knew you would." She squeezed my hand, and I felt a stab of guilt.

I heard a security guard's yells as he tried to clear the hallway. "I don't want you to be late for class. Let me walk you." I tugged on her hand.

We took a back stairway. Though we went fast, I couldn't outrun her questions. "That was so good of you to be there for his family. Do you think they suspected he was doing drugs?"

"His family thinks he was set up." Far as I knew, that was true. K-Ron's mom said so on *Larry King Live*.

"How sad. K-Ron has everything he could possibly want, and he's throwing it all away because of his addiction."

I rolled my eyes. "Gimme a break. Any nigga would give his right arm to trade places with K-Ron."

"Not *now*, I bet. It sounds like the charges are serious. Oops—this is my class."

"If K-Ron's lucky, he'll get off with probation and rehab."

"I hope so, for his sake and his family's."

Her sympathy for him made me sick, but I kept my cool, reminding myself that she didn't know any better.

"You better hurry to class," she said. "I'll see you at lunch?"

"Sure."

She held my hand a second longer. "I just want to say, K-Ron's family is lucky to have your support."

"Thanks." But I wanted to puke.

BREAKING THE RULES

THAT NIGHT AT NINE, I KNOCKED ON ALYSE'S DOOR, HALF AN hour late.

The door opened. Alyse pulled me inside, wrapped her arms around me, and kissed me. Her lips were irresistible. *Alyse* was irresistible.

"What a hello," I said.

"I've been wanting to do that all day."

I smiled down at her. "Then why didn't you?"

"Maybe I'm afraid for my safety."

"What do you mean?"

"C'mon, you know all the girls at school would love to get with you." She touched the diamond stud in my ear. "I don't want to show off the fact that we're together."

All I could think was, *We're together? Are we together?*

I felt good and panicked at the same time.

"Sorry I'm late. I got caught in the rain and had to go back and change."

"No problem. What do you say we do an hour of work, then chill for a little while? I've had a long day; bet you have too. Tomorrow night we'll get together earlier, say six, and finish the rest. If we don't have it done by Wednesday, Amullo's going to take off ten percent."

In the next hour we got a lot done. Alyse usually took charge when we worked on the project, but today she seemed out of it, and wanted me to make the decisions.

Later we closed up the books and went to the couch. Alyse curled into my side. I was gonna turn the TV on when she reached up and stopped me.

"No TV?"

"Not now."

"You okay, honey? You look tired."

She nodded against my side. "I am."

"You want me to go?"

"Not yet," she mumbled.

I stroked her hair. I didn't say nothing because I didn't think she wanted me to. Maybe she needed a few minutes of quiet. I was cool with that.

Suddenly she made a hiccuping noise. I looked down and saw her wiping her eyes.

"What's going on, boo?"

She pulled away from me. "N-nothing."

What was wrong with her? What was I supposed to do?

"Shh, don't cry." I pulled her against me, and let her cry against my chest. "Well, if you wanna cry, that's okay."

After a couple of minutes, she stopped. She got up, cleaned herself up in the bathroom, and came back.

"Ty, I'm sorry. I didn't want that to happen. When I'm tired, I sometimes get emotional."

It was more than being tired, I could tell. "You can cry all you want, I don't care about that." I smoothed her hair back from her forehead. "But I wanna know why."

She wouldn't look at me. "Mike called earlier tonight. He's Gavin's father."

"He bothering you?"

"Nah. He's just a loser. I don't want him to have anything to do with me or Gavin. I told him as long as he stays away from us, I won't take him to court for not paying child support."

"Did he agree to stay away?"

"Yeah." She sighed. "Hearing him on the phone reminds me of what an idiot I was."

"Everybody got regrets. You gotta put them behind you."

"Most of the time I do, but sometimes I can't. I messed everything up. I mean, how will I get into a good college with "Last Chance High" on my record?"

"The Alyse I know don't talk like that."

"The Alyse you know is the Alyse I show people. Now you're seeing the real thing."

"Good." I wrapped my arms around her. "I'm sick of you being Miss Perfect all the time."

"You're tripping," she said, hugging me back. "Ty . . ."

"What?"

"You're the best."

"I don't know about that."

"Well, I do." She raised her lips.

The passion in her kiss took me by surprise. I could feel how emotional she was.

Even as we kissed, I knew I was breaking one of my golden rules. *No relationships until I turn twenty-one.* But how could I turn away from something that felt so damn right?

I couldn't.

When the kiss was over, we held each other. I felt something I hadn't felt in a long time.

Happy. Just plain happy.

But soon, fear came creeping up behind it.

How long could I hold on to Alyse before she found out who I really was?

SHATTERED GLASS

THE NEXT NIGHT I LEFT THE GYM, MY MUSCLES TIGHT FROM A good workout. Stepping onto the wet dark streets, the smell of earthworms hit me. Poor suckers, the rain flooded their homes and forced them out to die in the streets.

My growling stomach couldn't wait until I got to the hotel. I walked into a Dominican restaurant and ordered dinner. I ate in five minutes flat. Then I went outside and walked toward Flatbush.

A car came around the corner, a little too slow.

Without thinking, I hit the pavement.

Shots cut through the air above me. My body went into overdrive. Rolling twice, I dove behind a mess of trash cans, covering my head as bullets ricocheted off metal. My arm burned. I knew I was hit.

I looked right and left for an escape. The door of a Chinese Laundromat was a few feet away. I made a run for it.

In two seconds, I was crashing inside. Everybody started screaming as bullets shattered the front windows. I heard the screech of tires, and the gunfire stopped.

I was on my knees, blood all over the white tile floor. Trying to catch my breath, I looked up to make sure they were gone. Then I passed out.

I didn't stay unconscious for long. I guess God wanted me to remember this day.

When I opened my eyes, two EMTs were bent over me. I groaned as they put pressure on my right arm and my stomach. Every breath meant more pain. Gritting my teeth, I focused on a piece of glass on the floor. *You gotta survive*, I told myself. *Be strong*.

A needle went into my arm, and in a few seconds, blackness.

For a long time I was in the dark. I knew that stuff was going on around me, but I couldn't wake up. I was too busy wrestling with the pain. I saw the lights of the operating room above me, and later, voices, some I knew, some I didn't.

I woke up in a hospital room. A fat black nurse was doing something to my arm. I moaned.

She looked at me. "Are you waking up, dear?"

"I . . . oww!"

"Sorry, honey. Your bandages have to be changed." I felt a pull, and turned my head to see what she was doing. When I saw the gooey, bloodstained bandage, I looked away.

"What's your name?" she asked me.

"Shouldn't you know that if you messing with me?"

"I know your name. I want to make sure you know it."

"It's Tyrone Johnson. I didn't get shot in the head or nothing."

"You better thank the good Lord for that! And thank Him the bullet in your abdomen wasn't an inch to the left."

I went silent, taking this in. I was still dealing with this life-and-death shit. I didn't need it thrown back in my face.

"You scare all the patients like this?"

"Just the ones I think should be scared. The ones I think are involved in gangs or drugs."

"You say that to every young black man?"

"Only the ones people *ain't* calling innocent bystanders. You might as well know, your first visitors will be the cops."

"Jesus."

She cleared her throat loud. "I'd appreciate it if you didn't take the Lord's name in vain."

"Sorry."

She pulled back the sheet to look at my stomach, bunching it in front of me so I couldn't see what was going on.

In the other bed on my side of the room, a middle-aged white guy was watching TV. An old man was sleeping in the far corner. The bed across from me was empty. Guess this was the best Mom's cheap-ass insurance could do.

I gasped. My wound stung like hell as she changed the bandage.

The pain sobered me up. I could so easily be in a body bag right now. My enemy took the step I didn't want to take, and that's why he almost won.

Almost.

The fist on my good arm tightened. This wasn't over.

Not by a long shot.

"There, it's done and everything's looking good." The nurse put the sheet back in place. "I have to call those officers and tell you you're awake. They'll be coming to ask you some questions."

"Fine," I grumbled. "I ain't going nowhere."

• • •

Two cops showed up stinking of coffee and cigarettes.

I recognized Akindele the minute he walked through the door. The guy with him, a white beanpole with a bushy mustache, walked up to the bed.

Time to get grilled. The guy next to me was gonna eat this up. He'd probably turned down the volume on his headphones.

"I'm Detective Scanlan. I understand you've met Detective Akindele. How are you feeling, Mr. Johnson?"

"Like I been shot." I didn't need no cops pretending to give a shit about how I was feeling.

Scanlan closed the curtain around the bed. Oh, I got it— our own little interrogation room.

"We don't want to encroach on your recovery time, Mr. Johnson. So the better you answer our questions, the sooner we'll leave."

"Shoot."

"Do you know who shot you?" Scanlan asked.

"Nope."

"Do you have any idea who could be behind it?"

"I must've been mistaken for somebody else."

Scanlan looked surprised. "You're calling it a random drive-by?"

"You got it." I closed my eyes and took a breath. All this talking was making me hurt worse.

"Please describe the car and anyone who might've been inside."

"They was shooting at me. I can't describe nothing."

Akindele stood at the foot of the bed. "We already have reliable descriptions of the car, but not of the assailants." Damn, the guy sounded like James Earl Jones. "We believe that the shooting is drug related. We suspect that you're a dealer, but we're not taking steps to prosecute you at this time. We would, however, like to prosecute whoever tried to kill you, but that's impossible without your help."

"I don't know what you talking about," I said. "This ain't no drug-related shooting."

Akindele curled his hands around the rail at the end of the bed. "What was it then?"

"I dunno."

"I would've thought you'd want to see justice done," Akindele said. "Not only for yourself, but for the other victims of this shooting."

"Other victims? What do you mean?"

The detectives looked at each other and shook their heads.

"What happened? Did other people get hurt?"

Scanlan turned to Akindele. "Thought you said this one had some brains in him."

"I thought so too. Let's go." Akindele opened the curtain. They headed for the door.

"Wait!" I shouted. "Tell me what happened—did somebody else get hurt?" I had to know.

"Read the paper," Scanlan said. "Good night, Mr. Johnson." He closed the door behind him.

I buzzed for help.

A young white nurse came in.

"Nurse, I need to know if anybody else got hurt when I got shot."

"I'm sorry, I don't know. Why don't you just have a rest and—"

"I wanna know what happened! Can't you get me a damn newspaper?"

"Please quiet down. I'll try to find one."

Minutes passed and nobody came. Shit, did everybody think that telling me the truth would freak me out?

The guy beside me kept glancing at me. Finally I shot him a *mind your business* glare. He turned away fast.

I couldn't stand it. Did someone get killed? An innocent nobody just doing their laundry or walking down the street?

It didn't matter, I told myself. If someone got hurt or died, it was a damn shame, but it wasn't my fault. I didn't ask for this to happen.

But somehow I *had* to know.

Another nurse came in—it was the *don't take the Lord's name in vain* one. She gave me a copy of the *Daily News*. "Page four." And left.

The headline: LAUNDROMAT SHOOTING IN BROOKLYN.

The picture: A Chinese woman hysterical in front of the shattered windows of the laundromat.

The caption: *Chun Wah Soo in despair as her newly opened Laundromat is damaged by gunfire.*

I started to read.

What began as a quiet Brooklyn evening was shattered when assailants in a black Toyota shot local teen Tyrone Johnson in what appeared to be a premeditated drive-by shooting.

"As soon as he came out of the restaurant, the car came around the corner, real slow like," said one witness, who requested not to be identified. "The shooting started, and the guy, he jumped behind them garbage cans. Then he ran into the Laundromat and that's when they shot up the place."

The people in the Soo Laundromat watched in horror as the bloody Johnson fell to the floor.

"It was terrifying," said Marg Walker, who had been doing laundry with her eight-year-old son. "We all thought the shooters might follow him in here to finish the job. And maybe finish us, too."

Tyrone Johnson sustained gunshot wounds to the arm and abdomen and is in stable condition after several hours of surgery. Five other victims had to be hospitalized for cuts and trauma inflicted by the shattering glass.

Police have not established a motive for the shooting, but neighbors speculate the shooting was drug related.

Johnson is the son of former Brooklyn drug kingpin Orlando Johnson.

Brooklyn City Councillor Jeffrey Benn says this shooting is only the latest act of violence in a string of drug- and gang-related incidents this year. . . .

I tossed the paper onto the bedstand. Nobody got killed, thank God. But my name was out.

Weird, but I was kind of relieved. No more lying, no more hiding.

No more Alyse.

I told myself it was for the best. If she was out of my life, I wouldn't have to worry that Darkman would find out about her and Gavin. Now that Darkman had tried to kill me, I had no choice but to stay away from them.

The article in the paper meant I didn't have to tell her myself.

I was a coward. A punk.

The nurse came in with a fruit basket. She put it on the bedstand and gave me the card.

"Strange time of night to be sending stuff, don't you think?"

"I guess."

I waited until she left before reading it.

Don't forget Daddy's advice.
Get well soon.

VISITING HOURS

THE NEXT MORNING I PISSED IN WHAT LOOKED LIKE A METAL vase and choked down some breakfast slop—all of this before Mom showed up.

"Hi, sweetie." She kissed the top of my head. I caught a whiff of that familiar mama-smell. "Is the pain real bad?"

"Nah."

"My poor son. Would you like some water?"

"Sure."

She lifted the cup and gave me the straw. "Before you know it, you'll be comfy at home. I'm'a take good care of you."

Uh-oh. No way I was going home when I got out of here. I had a business to run and Darkman to deal with. I couldn't do those things with Mom around.

She sat by the bed and started boring me with work and neighborhood stuff, like she would any other day. No questions about the shooting, about my dealing. Her strategy: Help me get well, *then* dog me out.

That was the thing about mamas. No matter how bad you fucked up, no matter how much they hated what you did, they were still going to be there for you.

I was glad. A little of Mom's TLC would do me good.

I managed to stay awake for an hour, but whatever drugs they gave me kept pulling me under.

"You need to sleep, sweetie," Mom said. "Would you like me to stay while you nap?"

"It's okay, Ma."

"I'll be back first thing tomorrow. If you need me in the meantime, call." She kissed my cheek and left.

Later on, my favorite nurse came in, looking mighty salty. "There's a real persistent young man out there who claims to be your brother, Jackson. He don't look anything like you, and he says he don't have ID." Her hands went to her hips. "He's gotten on my last nerve. I thought I'd let you choose if you want to see him. If not, we'll have Security take him out of here."

I smiled. Who else but Sonny? He wouldn't let no family-only rule get in his way. "Yeah, Jackson's my brother. I been missing him."

"If you're sure. That guy, he's crazy." She walked out.

Seconds later, "Yo, my dog! How you feeling?"

"A'ight."

"I was thinking I'd have to jump one of them orderlies for their uniform."

"Don't make me laugh, Sonny. It hurts too much."

"You ain't looking too bad. They say you lost a lot of blood, but after a few transfusions you were good to go."

"What?"

"Doctor said you got four pints."

"Four pints!"

"Don't sweat it—they always test the blood to make sure it's clean."

"Yeah, but . . . that's so weird to have someone else's blood in me. That's fucked up."

"What happened to you is what's fucked up. Everybody was scared shitless. And your mama, when she saw me, she came at me with her long-ass nails. Talk about O.D.in', man."

"She scratch you up?"

"Almost. I had to run like a mutherfucka. Anyway, 5-0's been hanging around. What you tell them?"

"Squat."

"So they don't—" Sonny broke off, and closed the curtains around the bed, as if the old man and the daughter who was feeding him gave a rat's ass. The guy next to me, luckily, was out walking the halls. "They don't know about Darkman?"

I lowered my voice too. "Nah, it's us they wanna take down. You should've seen them try to guilt me into spilling my guts, making me think other people got shot. Anyway, be careful what you say around here."

"I hear you. By the way, that chick you introduced me to, she been here a few times."

"*Alyse?*"

"Yeah. She mad quiet. She was asking doctors and nurses how you doing. She came earlier today, wanting to see you, but they wouldn't let her 'cause she wasn't family."

"If you see her again, tell her to go home. Tell her I'll call her."

"Sho 'nuff. So, what are we gonna do about this?" He leaned over the bed and whispered, "I know a few niggas who'd get rid of Darkman for a fee."

"I got it covered."

"No offense, but you said that before, and look where you at."

"I know who I'm gonna hire. I'll call him as soon as I get outta here."

"Gimme his number. I'll call him today."

I thought about it, but my instincts told me to hold off. "Not now. It's too soon. 5-o will see it as revenge."

"Sure, but like you said, they got no proof. If you trust this nigga to do a clean job, why wait?"

"Because . . . because I wanna be there," I lied.

"Then I wanna be there too. Anyone who goes after my brotha's gotta go down hard."

THE BREAK

THE NEXT DAY, ANYBODY COULD VISIT, AND ANYBODY DID.
Like Cheddar and Bear, who said they cut school just to
see me—I knew they'd be cutting, anyway. I wondered if
Alyse would show up, but I knew that if she did, it would
be after school.

Around seven o'clock, in walked Mr. Guzman. "Ty, how
are you doing?"

I straightened in bed. "I'm good."

"Glad to hear it." He pulled up a chair. "Everyone's hoping you'll be back at school soon."

"So I ain't getting kicked out?"

"Why would you be?"

Was he playing or what? "You read the papers, Mr.
Guzman. You know what they saying about me."

Mr. Guzman wasn't fazed. "I don't know how much, if any, of what the papers have written is true. Frankly, it doesn't concern me." He took a thick folder out of his bag and put it on the bedstand. "All of your teachers have provided me with materials so you can keep up in their classes. Depending on how long your recovery takes, we may be able to arrange a tutor."

"I don't need a tutor, Mr. Guzman. Thanks, but I got other things on my mind."

"I'll leave the folder here. Have a look at it when you're feeling better. My phone number is in there if you have questions."

"Okay."

He got up. "We all want to see you succeed, Ty."

"Thanks, Mr. Guzman."

He left, and I stared at the ceiling. As if I'd be thinking about school at a time like this. I had other things to worry about—like making sure Sonny was on top of things, and figuring out what Darkman was gonna do next.

"Ty."

My throat went dry as Alyse approached the bed, sad eyes sliding over me. "How are you?"

"A'ight."

"You really scared me." She touched my arm. Her hand was so warm. "I prayed you'd be okay."

"Thanks. Looks like your prayers worked."

"I can see that." She smiled softly. "I saw Mr. Guzman outside. It was nice of him to come, don't you think? He really doesn't want you to fall behind."

"Yeah."

There was an awkward silence.

"Could you close the curtain?" I asked. The guy in the next bed was talking on the phone to his wife, but I didn't like how he kept looking over.

"Sure." Then she cleared her throat and said quietly, "People are saying that you got shot because you were involved in drug dealing, that it's the family business."

I swallowed.

"I don't blame you for not telling me about your dad."

"I ain't ashamed of my dad."

"I'm not asking you to be. I don't think it's fair that people are judging you based on what your dad did. You got shot, they don't know who did it, so they're making *you* look like a criminal."

I couldn't believe it. Even with all the rumors, Alyse thought I was innocent. Was my act that good?

She squeezed my hand. "I'm so glad you're okay."

I was tempted, real tempted, to keep her believing in me. The last thing I wanted to do was hurt her. But I had no choice. For her safety and Gavin's, she needed to stay away from me. And I was tired of playing her this way.

"Alyse, you gonna hate me."

"What? Why would I hate you?"

I listened. The guy next to me was still on the phone. I lowered my voice. "I took over my dad's business. I'm a hustler, and it ain't small scale. That's why I got shot. I got shot because somebody wanted my territory."

I wanted to look away, but I didn't. My punishment was seeing the look on her face as I told her the truth. "I know I should've told you a long time ago, but I was selfish. I knew you wouldn't be down with it, and I didn't wanna lose you."

She yanked her hand away. "You're fucking insane. You put me and my son in danger!"

"Listen, after I found out that somebody was making a play for my business, I never took you out in public. You gotta know I never put you in danger."

"And I thought we didn't go out because you didn't want me to spend money on a babysitter!"

"I know I shouldn't have started up with you in the first

place. But I wanted to be with you so bad. I'm sorry, Alyse. I'm mad sorry."

"I stood up for you. Now the whole school is laughing at me!"

"Alyse . . ." I reached for her hand, but she kept it away from me. "We both know that our relationship's gotta stop here. Even if you were willing to give me another chance, the situation's too dangerous for me to have a girlfriend. But we can still keep in touch. I'll call you."

"Are you serious?" She looked at me like I was a monster. "You played me. That ain't no basis for a friendship. That ain't no basis for anything!"

She walked out.

ON THE HUNT

A WEEK LATER, I LEFT THE HOSPITAL ON MY OWN TWO FEET.

I called Mom when I knew she was at work and left a message. "Hey, Mom. I'm out of the hospital and I'm going back to my friend's place. I need some time to myself to think about things, so I don't wanna come home just yet. Hope you understand. I'll call you soon. Love ya."

I cringed at the thought of how she'd react to the message, but it had to be.

I moved to another hotel, where I checked in under a fake name. Monfrey was hanging on to my stuff from the first hotel. The new hotel, in Bay Ridge, was a perfect place to lie low while I got my strength back.

My first visitor was Monfrey.

He came in, plunking down my duffel bag and looking like he wanted to hug me. "Ty, man, you look good."

I knew he was lying. I lost a few pounds in the hospital— muscle I'd worked hard to put on.

"I wanted to visit you in the hospital, but I didn't wanna risk blowing my cover."

"You did the right thing. Sit down, Monfrey. Help yourself to some eats." I had chips and chocolate from the vending machine. Monfrey was always hungry, maybe because he was always stoned. From the way he was walking, I could tell it had been a heavy few days for him.

He didn't go right for the chips. Talking mattered more. "When I heard what went down, I almost put a cap in Kevin's bitch-ass myself. But when I found out you didn't die, I figured you'd want to take care of that yourself."

"You're right. I want you doing just what you doing. I need you on top of your game."

"I had no idea it was gonna happen, Ty. Kevin didn't tell the guys, or if he did, he told them one-by-one, and made them keep it on the down-low. That day Kevin came in, all cocky and shit. But when he found out that you wasn't nec- essarily gonna die, he wilded out."

"I won't make the same mistake, Monfrey. I'm hiring a professional—somebody who don't make mistakes."

"I hear that. It's the only way. Kevin *will* come after you again. He got even more to prove now, since he fucked up the first time."

"Did you get any closer to Crow?"

"Close enough to know it's only a matter of time before he gets on a plane to Miami and leaves Kevin in the dust."

"What about the other guys?"

"Kevin's still got them under control—for now."

"I'll pass on your digits to the guy I'm hiring. He'll be calling you to get the goods on Kevin's routine." I cracked my knuckles. "Kevin King ain't gonna live to see the new year."

When Monfrey left, I called Ronnie. He told me to come over ASAP.

2513 Nostrand Avenue was a redbrick townhouse. When the cab stopped at the curb I saw a curtain pull back in the front room. A little girl stood there and waved.

A hitman with kids.

I walked up to the door and rang the bell. The girl opened the inner door, looking up at me with big eyes. Behind her I heard heavy footsteps.

"Stephanie, I told you never to answer the door by yourself!" The man who walked up behind her was big-boned, maybe forty, with a beard that was going gray. He opened the screen door and shook my hand. "Come on in."

The hallway had family pictures all over the walls. It would've been less strange to meet Ronnie in a back alley or deserted parking lot.

"Nice place you got."

Ronnie smiled, flashing gold teeth. "Thank you. No mortgage or nothing. Meet my daughter, Stephanie."

"Hi, Stephanie. I'm Ty." I shook the small hand that reached up to me.

Ronnie patted her head. "We going to my office, honey. Keep on watching *The Lion King*."

She ran off.

Ronnie motioned for me to follow him downstairs. "My wife's at Ronnie Jr.'s basketball game. They won't be back no time soon."

The basement had been converted into an office. By the looks of the stuffed bookshelves and half-open filing cabinets, Ronnie had another job—or did a good job of faking it.

"Sit down. Boy, you the image of yo' daddy."

"I been told that a time or two." I sat down in the leather chair in front of the desk.

"Tell me about the job."

I explained the Darkman situation as best I could.

Ronnie said, "I do a clean job, Ty. I got a wife and kids, a good job with ConEd, and I *ain't* going to jail. So I take a shot only if I can do it right, and if I can't, I find another chance."

"How much?"

"Ten Gs. Five now, five when the job's done."

"A'ight. I guess you gonna tail him a few times before you make the hit?"

"That's the way I do it. I need a solid week to watch him."

"I got a guy on the inside who can help with all the details." I passed him a piece of paper with Monfrey's name and phone number.

His eyes lit up like he got an early Christmas present. "That'll be very helpful."

In my pocket, I had an envelope of cash. I counted out five thousand on the desk. "Call me before you make the hit, so I can have a good alibi."

"Of course. I'll give you plenty of warning. I guess you worried he'll come after you again?"

"I ain't worried. I got my own back."

Ronnie smiled. "*Damn*, boy, you just like yo' daddy."

Back in the hotel, I got a call on my cell. I recognized the number.

"Alyse?"

"Hi. I'm sorry to bother you. It's just that all of our teachers have been bugging me about where you are. They say you can't be reached at your mom's. The school doesn't have your cell number, and I didn't think you'd want me to give it to them."

"Thanks for that."

"Anyway, I said I'd call to ask if and when you're coming back to Les Chancellor and if you need work to be assigned. So . . . are you coming back?"

"I'll be honest with you, Alyse. I got other things to worry about. Life-and-death things."

I heard her take a breath. "Ty . . ." She was trying not to cry, I could hear it in her voice. "Can't you get out of all this?"

"It ain't simple like that." I wished I could find the words to explain everything to her, to show her that I wasn't the bad guy she thought I was. "I'm doing what I gotta do to survive."

She was silent. And then, quietly, "I don't want you to die."

"I'll be all right. Tell them at school I ain't coming back."

Damn, it sounded final. But there was no way I could handle school when I was in the middle of this shit. No way.

"Why not?"

"I got other plans."

"Like what?"

"It don't matter."

"Ty . . ."

"What?"

"Nothing."

"Do you miss me, boo?" I asked. "Because I miss you."

"I—I don't wanna hear that."

"Well, it's true."

And maybe I wanted to hear that you missed me, too.

She sniffed. "I'll tell them at school that you're not coming back, if you're sure that's what you want."

"It's what I want."

"Fine. I better go now. Oh, by the way, I presented our Alice Walker project."

"How'd we do?"

"We got an A."

"We were a good team, weren't we?"

"Yeah. We were."

RETURN TO PARADISE

GOING BACK TO THE STREETS WAS NO PICNIC. I WAS always looking over my shoulder. Part of me wished I was flat on my back again so I didn't have to deal with the streets yet.

I was glad to get out of Brooklyn for a few hours to see Jimmy Pennington on the Upper West Side. The doorman in Jimmy's swanky building had to let me through, but suspicious eyes followed me all the way to the elevator.

One day, when I had a decent job to cover me, I'd live in a building like this. I'd be in the penthouse.

Getting off on the nineteenth floor, I knocked on Jimmy's door. I heard movement inside, but a long time passed before the door opened.

Jimmy peered around the door with bloodshot eyes. He

looked scary. "Fuck, man, I'm glad to see you. You're saving my fucking life."

"Y'all right, Jimmy?"

"No. I'm in hell. Come in."

I walked in. "What's going on? Looks like a tornado ripped through this place."

"I'm trying to get my stuff together. I have to move." He sat down on the couch. From the look and smell of him, he hadn't changed his clothes or showered in days. "Sit down. Talk to me, Johnson. I'd get you a beer, but the fridge is empty."

"I can't stay, I got another delivery. Where's your girl-friend?" I couldn't for the life of me remember her name.

"Bitch is gone. Doesn't matter. Let's do a hit."

"You got the dough?"

Jimmy looked up at me, and for a crazy second I thought he was gonna cry. "Look, Johnson, I don't have it this time. I lost my job. They found out I was selling. Said they wouldn't press charges if I went quietly. They don't need half the firm's habit exposed in the papers."

"Shit. Sorry, man." I almost asked what he was gonna do now, but I held back. That wasn't my business. Orlando always warned me not to make a customer's personal life my business.

"Lend me twenty grand worth and I'll sell it." He was wringing his hands. "I still got my customers. I promise I can sell it."

"Sorry, Jimmy. I can't give you the stuff without the cash. It's policy. I gotta go." I stood up and headed for the door. He followed me into the hallway, where I pushed for the elevator.

"You gotta be kidding me, Johnson! After all I done for you, it's, 'tough luck, man, go fuck yourself'? Please gimme a chance."

"I can't." Tick tick tick. Where the hell was the elevator?

"Then gimme a hit. Just to get me through the night. Please."

"The last thing you need right now is coke, Jimmy."

"Oh, c'mon, Johnson." He grabbed my arm. "You've gotta help me out."

I smelled how desperate he was. I knew what he was thinking—if he landed a few quick punches, maybe it would give him the chance to grab the coke and run.

I stared him down, letting him know without words that he didn't have a chance. Then I looked at his hand. "Back off."

His hand dropped. The elevator came. I got on.

"Ty, I'm begging you."

But he didn't stop the doors from closing.

I sucked in a breath, staring at the numbers as the elevator went down. I never would've thought that would happen to Jimmy. Never.

I passed a hand over my sweaty forehead.

You did the right thing, I told myself.

You did the right thing.

THE MEETING

OVER THE NEXT FEW DAYS I KEPT IN CLOSE CONTACT WITH Ronnie, who was tracking Darkman's movements. Any day now he'd call to tell me the job was about to be done. I already decided that my alibi would be playing pool with homies.

And then I got a call that changed everything.

"Ty, it's Monfrey. You wouldn't believe all the shit going down."

"What's happening?"

"I caught Crow and Leanne in bed. Nigga, you should've seen it. They was begging me not to tell Kevin. Begging me! I said, what's in it for me? They said cash. Said they been planning to clean Kevin out and bounce."

"They *told* you this? How'd they know they could trust you?"

"They got no choice. If I snitch about finding them in

bed, Kevin would kill them, anyway. Ty, they wanna bring Kevin down as bad as we do. I think we can make a deal."

"Monfrey, I'm relying on your instincts here. Do they really want to see him lose everything?"

"They hate his guts. Trust me. Let me set up a meeting. You'll see for yourself."

"Do it, then. Set it up."

The meeting was the same day at four. In the meantime I called Ronnie's cell. The voice mail picked up. "Ronnie, yo, I just wanted to say, don't make a move yet. Hold off, I'm working on something. I'll get back to you."

I showed up at the Promenade by the Brooklyn Bridge at two minutes to four. Too wired to sit down, I shoved my hands in my pockets and walked. I left my jacket open so I could feel the cold wind.

I saw Monfrey coming up the block. With his nappy Afro, he was hard to miss. He was with a man and a woman. I walked in their direction, keeping my head up and my eyes on them. I wanted them to pick up on my confidence.

When they got closer, Monfrey waved. I nodded back.

Crow was tall and skinny, with long dreadlocks in a ponytail. Leanne wore a fur coat and stiletto heels.

Monfrey introduced, "Crow, Leanne, this is Ty."

"You look young," Leanne said.

I looked her straight in the eye. "You got nothing to worry about."

Crow said, "Monfrey here tells us you might be interested in working out a strategy to bring Kevin King down."

"Tell me what you got in mind," I said.

"The way we see it, we all got the same problem: *Kevin*. We wanna see him locked up."

"So you'll help set him up?"

Crow nodded. "We can get him picked up with a trunk full of rock. Enough to bring him down for fifteen years at least."

"Sounds like a plan to me," I said. *Almost too good to be true*. "So why do you need me?"

Leanne said, "We deliver Kevin, and you help us out."

"How much?"

She cracked her gum. "It ain't money we need. We'll clean out Kevin's accounts just before he gets arrested. We want a slice of Brooklyn. *Your* Brooklyn." She looked at Crow, who nodded for her to keep going. "We know you got a few customers in Bed-Stuy and Brownsville, but you don't do most of your business there. We want you to give us those customers, and put the word out that we got the best shit in the hood."

Crow went on, "We been thinking, you ain't doing too much business in those areas, probably 'cause you don't wanna spread yourself too thin. If you give up that territory, we won't cause you no problems. We ain't over-ambitious people. But we want to live well, and we can do that if you cut us this deal."

"It ain't just about spreading myself too thin," I said. "Crips are in control of most of those hoods. You heard of Trigger?"

Crow nodded. "Leader of the Brownsville Crips. Kevin been trying to get Trigger to help him put you out of business for months, but Trigger won't do it. He says your family is Honorary Crip."

I also had peeps who called me Honorary Blood, but I kept that on the down-low. Though Crow wasn't rocking colors right now, I knew that Kevin and his gang were true blue.

"Me and Trigger, we cool," I said. "If I wanted to give up my territory to you, he'd have nothing to say about it. But if you wanted to expand onto his turf, that's between you and him."

"I got you," Crow said. "So you like our offer?"

"I'll think about it," I said.

"Okay, but don't take too long. We're getting a shipment in three days—it'd be a perfect setup."

"What about the other guys who work for him? They loyal?"

"Only because they gotta be," Crow answered. "Kevin don't take care of his people, he don't treat them with respect."

Leanne said, "You know why he left Miami? He couldn't stand being the youngest son with the smallest cut in his brothers' business. He started stealing cash from them, cheating his own brothers! When they found out, they told him to pack his bags. So instead of crawling into a hole, he come up here thinking he gonna be big-time."

"He pays his men shit because he says he ain't got no money, but that's bullshit," Crow added.

Leanne lifted her chin. "I know what he got in the bank. I know his PIN, I know everything. His money will keep us living real nice for a while."

"You gonna let us know if it's a go?" Crow said.

"I made up my mind," I said. "It's a go."

When the meeting was over, I called Ronnie again. This time he picked up.

"Ronnie? It's me, Ty."

"Ty, now what's this about stalling? What's the problem?"

"I don't need you anymore. But keep the money I gave you for your time."

"You don't need me? Now why's that?"

"I found a better way to take him down."

"Like what?"

"The cops are gonna do it for free."

"Don't tell me you working with the po-po."

"I ain't. But Kevin King's gonna get set up good."

"You sure?"

"Yeah. I'd be stupid not to go with it. I know you gone to a lot of trouble. Like I said, keep the five grand."

"A'ight. Watch yourself. And if you need me, call."

"Thanks, Ronnie."

I hung up, then speed-dialed Sonny.

He answered, "What up?"

"We gotta talk. There's been a change of plan. Can you meet me at La Tranquilla?"

"You got it."

I grabbed a yellow cab.

Half an hour later, I met Sonny in front of the restaurant.

"You look good, son," he said. "You recovering mad quick."

"Thanks. I can see you put on a few pounds yourself. Thanksgiving turkey?"

"Nah, it's all muscle." Sonny touched a bicep, proud.

"You been using that new protein powder I showed you?"

"Damn straight. It don't taste too bad with o.j. But all those eggs, boy"—he made a face—"they make me burp nasty."

"You'll get used to it. You wanna bulk up, you need a shit-load of protein."

When we walked into the restaurant, we were greeted by the hostess Jeanine and a roomful of stares. Even the black couple gave us *What you doing here?* looks.

As she led us to our table, I nudged Sonny. "Why don't we get us dinner jackets sometime? Pretend we big-shot lawyers or something."

"That wouldn't be no fun! I like to see the look on their faces. They be wondering why we ain't at McDonald's."

We sat down, and Sonny leaned over the table. "So what's this about a change of plan?"

"Let's order first. I don't wanna get interrupted."

Sonny opened the menu and looked it over like he ain't seen it a dozen times before.

The waiter came up. "Good evening. Have you had a chance to peruse our wine selection, sirs?" I couldn't tell if he was gay or just British. Maybe both.

Sonny answered, "Being traditional guys, we'll go for Dom Pérignon. We celebrating my boy Ty's good health."

"Indeed? Good health is always a cause for celebration."

Sonny nodded. "Not just anybody gets shot twice in a drive-by and lives to tell about it."

It was worth it just to see the shock on the waiter's face. "Oh—oh dear."

I had to bite my lip to keep from laughing.

"I have a question for you," Sonny said to the waiter. "Which of these got the most protein? As you can see, I'm a brotha who cares about his physique. You can tell, right?"

"Undoubtedly."

"So which one: the salmon, the chicken parm, the filet mignon, or the penne with sausage?"

The waiter answered, "All of those dishes have plenty of protein, sir, so you should ask your palate for its preference."

"Just gimme the filet mignon, then."

"Excellent." The waiter turned to me. "And for you, sir?"

"I'll have the baked salmon."

The waiter came back soon after with the champagne.

I sipped it slow. "As I said, there's been a change of plan. We ain't hiring that guy no more."

Sonny almost choked on his Dom Pérignon. "The hell you talking about?"

"I got a better way to deal with Darkman."

"Like what?"

I explained that we now had an alliance with Crow and Leanne, and a plan to set Darkman up.

"Man, he tried to *kill you*. An eye for an eye, you know! Orlando said it himself!"

"This ain't Orlando's decision."

"Right. It's ours, and *you* made it by yourself. And you got me wondering, what are Crow and Leanne getting outta all this? You promise them something?"

"A few customers in Bed-Stuy and Brownsville, that's all."

"*What?*"

"Hey, keep it down."

"I don't get you, man. From the start of this Darkman shit, you was always stalling to do what you gotta do. You said you had a plan, and where did that get you? Shot. And now, when we about to finish this thing once and for all, you backing out!"

"I think it's a better plan. What if Ronnie gets caught and gives up my name? I don't wanna risk that."

"That's bullshit. Your daddy, *he* always did what he had to do."

"And he also landed his ass in jail. You lucky he didn't land *your* ass in jail too."

Sonny was shaking his head. "Man, I used to think you was smarter than him. But now, when I look at how you been dealing with Darkman, I think you just scared."

"Scared? I took two bullets and I'm still on top of my game. I ain't scared, but I'm tryna be smart. Why risk snuffing someone if you don't have to?"

"What do you think Orlando's gonna say when you tell him you cut this deal?"

"I ain't telling him yet. He'll find out after it's all gone down."

"He's gonna flip out when he hears that you gave up territory. You got no right making a deal like that."

"C'mon, we weren't planning on doing much in those hoods. Not with Trigger's Crips there."

"That ain't my point. My point is that we partners, and you shouldn't have made that decision without me. Especially a decision that could land you on a slab."

"I ain't going down from Darkman's bullets. My plan will work, I promise you."

"It better. 'Cause in this deal, you on your own."

THE BEST-LAID PLANS

AT THIS TIME OF YEAR, MOST GUYS MY AGE WERE COUNTING down to the Christmas holidays.

I was counting down to Judgment Day, the day of Darkman's downfall.

The night before Judgment Day I met with Monfrey and Crow. Leanne was at a Nets game with Darkman.

The meeting place was the top level of an East Village café. I bought coffee and went upstairs to the lounge. The atmosphere was totally pimp, with red velvet furniture and low lighting. Hip-hop tunes spun in the background, just loud enough to cover our conversation.

I saw Crow and Monfrey at the back of the lounge near a fireplace. I pulled up a chair and took out my Palm Pilot. "Let's go over the plan."

Crow pushed a dreadlock out of his face. "First thing tomorrow, I'll call Kevin and tell him I can't go on the pick-up."

"What's your excuse?"

"Food poisoning. I'm barfing and shitting every five minutes. I got spray from a joke store that really stinks like shit, so the guys won't suspect nothing."

"Kevin only asked you and Alejandro to go, right?"

"Yeah. Didn't need Natty."

"Good. Monfrey?"

He grinned at me.

"Monfrey? You stoned?"

"Maybe." Monfrey shrugged. "Tomorrow I'll wait for a call to tell me Darkman's gone. Then I'll help Leanne and Crow clear out the crib."

"Right. If drugs or guns or anything suspicious is found there, Leanne could get charged. What are you gonna do after that, Monfrey?"

"I'll say bye to them by nine thirty and hit the road."

"Right. You can help them out some in the morning, then you get outta there."

I turned to Crow. "What's your excuse to leave the apartment?"

"I'll tell Natty I'm going to see a doctor."

"Good idea. Now gimme a time line."

"Kevin and Alejandro are meeting the suppliers at nine thirty, but I don't know where. Kevin always keeps the location to himself. If you wanna be safe, be waiting outside by eight thirty."

"Do they change the place every time?"

"Yeah. Last time it was down on Coney Island. Time before that, it was in a Wal-Mart parking lot in Islip."

"I'll stay on his tail. Another thing. Do you think Natty will testify against Darkman and Alejandro?"

"He'll do whatever it takes to stay outta jail. If that means testifying against Kevin, he'll do it. He's tight with Alejandro, though, so he'll probably blame it all on Kevin."

"Fine with me."

We slapped hands.

JUDGMENT DAY

I WOKE UP AT 6:58 A.M., TWO MINUTES BEFORE MY ALARM WAS set to go off. It was a good sign. This was the day Darkman was gonna go down in flames, and I'd be there to watch.

I noticed my cell blinking and listened to the message.

"Yo, it's Sonny. It's one in the morning. I guess you getting some rest since everything's going down tomorrow morning. Look, I know you pissed off at me 'cause of how I reacted to the plan, but let's forget about that shit. I wanna come with you, back you up. So call me, I got my phone on."

I called him right back.

He answered, "Ty?"

"It's me. I'll meet you at Hertz on Bedford in forty-five minutes. We'll pick up the car and go for coffee. I'll catch you up on the plan."

"A'ight."

The car service got me to Hertz rental car at 7:45 a.m. sharp. Sonny was waiting for me outside.

"Sure you don't wanna take my car?" he asked.

"We can't risk Darkman recognizing it."

"I hear you."

A few minutes later we walked out of the building with the keys to a red Honda Civic. "I'll drive," I said.

"Be my guest. I'll be in charge of the ra-di-o." He yawned. "When we getting that coffee?"

"When we in Bed-Stuy. Let's do the parkway now, in case there's delays."

There was mad construction on the parkway, so I was glad we started out early. I gave Sonny a play-by-play of what I went over with Crow and Monfrey last night.

I turned onto Utica Avenue. Traffic was thick, but moving forward. Sonny put on 103.5, and I nodded my head to the bass.

"Was Desarae pissed off that I called so early?" I asked.

Sonny turned down the volume. "She always pissed off in the morning, it don't matter what time it is. We got a policy: We don't talk until after breakfast. But sometimes I can soften her up with a little morning nookie, know what I'm saying?"

"You got yourself a fine woman, Sonny."

He smiled. "I'm a lucky mutherfucka, ain't I?"

By 8:05 a.m., we pulled into a Dunkin' Donuts in Bed-Stuy. I parked at the far end of the lot on the off chance that Darkman stopped here too. Sonny ran in and brought out the coffee.

I was halfway through my coffee when my cell rang.

9-1-1 Crow.

I answered the phone. "What's going on?"

"Kevin wants me to go with them on the pickup."

"What? Don't he know how sick you are?"

"Kevin don't care. He's suspicious. If I don't go, he'll know something's up. *Shit!*"

"Calm down, Crow, we'll figure this out. If he wants you to go, then go."

"Go?"

"Just listen. You go with him to make the exchange, and on the way back, you tell him you got the shits and he gotta pull in somewhere. You go inside, then run out a back door and get the hell outta there. I'll have the cops there in five minutes. Kevin'll still have the stuff on him."

"What if Kevin comes looking for me?"

"He'll think you sick in the bathroom. Don't you think that'll buy you five or ten minutes?"

"Guess so."

"Leanne and Monfrey can clean out the crib without you. You just gotta relax. The plan's changed, but it'll still work. Remember, make him pull over ASAP after the pickup, because if you get too close to home, he could tell you to wait till you get there. Let him know he has to let you out or you'll shit in the car."

"When I get away, you'll pick me up?"

"Yeah, just call and tell me where you at. I'm in a red Honda Civic."

"Okay."

We hung up.

"Crow's going on the pickup?"

I leaned back against the seat. "Yeah, he can't do nothing about it. But I think the plan can still work."

"I hope this Crow nigga is good under pressure."

"Me too."

A few minutes later, we were sitting on the corner of Darkman's block. We saw Alejandro and Crow drive up, park in a visitor's space, and go inside.

We waited. Sonny drummed on the dashboard. After ten minutes, Darkman's silver Lexus drove out from behind the building.

I dipped the car into traffic.

The Lexus headed for the Manhattan Bridge. I stayed three cars behind and in the right-hand lane, close enough to keep an eye on him, far enough that he wouldn't know it.

After the bridge, Darkman turned west and drove along the waterfront. I wasn't surprised the deal was going down in this area. We met shipments here, too, sometimes.

"They slowing down," Sonny said.

"Take a look at the place when we drive past."

We drove by, then I made a left turn and parked the car. "Stay here, I'll be back in a few. All I need is a look to know the deal's going down. I don't need to get close."

"You be back in five minutes or—"

"You'll come save me. Thanks."

I crossed the street and jogged along the boardwalk. A group of South American workers played hacky sack on the pier. I walked onto the property, cool like I owned it, then jumped a fence, landing behind a storage shed. I looked around the side.

The silver Lexus was there, only ten feet from a green Camry. Alejandro, all three hundred pounds of him, leaned against the Lexus with his arms crossed while Darkman talked to a short, hairy Latino guy. Behind the

Latino guy was two thugs, almost as big as Alejandro.

It was the first time I set eyes on Darkman. He looked like any brother on the street—hair in cornrows, snorkel jacket—except that this brother tried to kill me.

I checked out the area. Crow was off to the far right, holding on to the guardrail, looking into the icy water. At one point he doubled over and started coughing. Then he slowly walked back toward the cars, his hand on his stomach.

Good acting, man.

Darkman didn't pay Crow no mind. He snapped his fingers at Alejandro, who opened up a briefcase. The Latino guy peeked in, nodded, and signaled his guys to open the trunk of the Camry.

The shipment was in two suitcases. Crow opened Darkman's trunk, and he and Alejandro fit the suitcases in.

I saw all I needed to see.

I climbed over the fence and jogged back to where Sonny waited. I banged on Sonny's window.

"*Damn*, son! You gave me a heart attack," he said as I got into my seat.

"Ain't my fault you was looking the wrong way." I started the engine.

"Saw the deal?"

"You bet."

I swung the car back onto South Street, heading north, then turned on a side street and switched off the engine.

"Now we wait. We're halfway between the pickup spot and the bridge. Crow's gonna get them to pull over somewhere around here."

I took out a map and gave it to Sonny. "We're right here, see? The pickup was here, and the bridge, you can see where it is. When he calls, I'll tell you the place and you gimme directions."

"A'ight."

I took another sip of coffee, cold by now. I didn't need caffeine when I had so much adrenaline pumping through my blood.

All I needed was for Crow to call.

I held on to my cell phone.

The car started to get cold. I put the heat on for a couple minutes, then turned it off again. I didn't need the car stalling on me.

The call came.

"Crow?"

"Ty! I'm in the bathroom at Basha Gas Station, on the

corner of Dover and Front Street. There's a Carvel and a McDonald's half a block away. Got that?"

"Basha Gas Station, Dover and Front. Got it. The cops'll be there soon. I'll meet you in the McDonald's parking lot."

We hung up. I called 9-1-1.

"Emergency center."

"I just saw a big drug deal go down outside Basha Gas Station, on Dover and Front."

"Are you sure about this?"

"Positive. I'm from Flatbush, lady. I know what a deal looks like."

"Can you describe the people involved?"

"Yeah, there was a big fat guy, and another guy wearing a blue snorkel jacket. He's got a silver Lexus parked at the gas station with Florida plates."

"I'm dispatching the police. Where are you located now, sir?"

"I'm on my cell a block away. Me and my cousin saw the whole thing. Them fools shouldn't be pulling that shit out in the open like that. Excuse my language, ma'am. My cousin's only eight. He don't need to see that."

"Sir, are the suspects still at the gas station?"

"I think so. The Lexus is still there."

"Do you know if the suspects are armed?"

"Hustlers is always strapped. Tell the cops to be careful." I hung up.

By now, I was driving. Sonny told me to turn right. I did, rounding the corner too close and screeching the tires.

"Go straight through the next two sets of lights. Wait, it's only one—turn!"

I turned onto Dover Street and spotted Basha Gas Station right away. I slowed down. "We gonna drive past it. Tell me if you see Darkman and Alejandro."

I coasted by the station at a relaxed speed. Sonny said, "A guy's smoking outside the car. Don't know if it's Darkman or Alejandro."

"He look three hundred pounds?"

"No."

"Then it's Darkman. There's nobody in the car?"

"No."

I parked in the McDonald's lot.

"Maybe Alejandro went inside to buy something, or he went to the bathroom," Sonny said.

"Maybe."

A gunshot.

Sonny and I looked at each other.

"*What the fuck?*" we shouted at the same time.

I opened the car door. Sonny grabbed my arm. "You fucking crazy? You don't wanna get in the middle of whatever's going down."

"Crow might need help."

As soon as I got out, I felt someone practically jump on my back. I let out a shout and swung around. It was a sweaty-faced Crow.

"Get me outta here, Ty."

"Get in the back, and *get down!*"

I jumped into the driver's seat.

"Sonny, meet Crow." I started the engine and swung out of the parking lot.

A muffled voice came from the back. "I shot Alejandro. *Fuck!*"

"What happened?" I asked over my shoulder.

"After I called you, I left the bathroom. I was gonna bounce, but Alejandro stopped me and asked where the fuck I was going. I told him I had to run, and he should too. He tried to grab me. I had to shoot him. Then I took off running. Thank God you was here."

"Don't thank God yet," I said. "Maybe nobody saw you. That means they'll think Darkman did it."

He breathed heavy. "I have to get outta town. I can't risk going down for shooting Alejandro."

"Is he dead?"

"I don't know. He was bleeding a lot. I shot him in the stomach. I didn't want to, but his stomach's so fucking huge and I didn't have a chance to aim. Ty, you gotta take me to the airport."

"I'll take you."

"Thanks, man." I heard him using his cell phone. "Leanne, honey, things didn't go so good. Alejandro came after me and—listen, just listen, I shot him. Baby, he was attacking me! Shh-shh . . . I'll explain later. Meet me at JFK. You been to the bank already? Great. Meet me at the Air Jamaica desk at JFK. Love ya."

Crow sat up in the back. "I hope you understand, man, I can't stick around, not after what I did." He put his face in his hands.

"Easy, Crow, you'll get on a plane just fine." But it wasn't Crow I was worried about. I was thinking about Darkman. Did they catch him with the drugs? If he ran when he heard the gunshot, would they be able to trace the car to him?

It took forty minutes to get to the airport. I dropped Crow off at Terminal 4.

"I'm good from here," Crow said. "Thanks." He leaned forward and squeezed my shoulder, then got out.

On the ride back, we flicked from one radio station to another, trying to find some local news. The airwaves were filled with dumbass Christmas jingles.

Finally we got lucky. "*. . . victim's name has not yet been released pending notification of his family. After a car chase in Lower Manhattan, the suspect was arrested with a sizable amount of narcotics.*"

I slammed the wheel. "That's gotta be him! Darkman's locked up!"

We howled and cheered.

"He won't see the light of day till he's old and gray, if he survives that long," Sonny said. "They'll get him for drug possession with the intention of dealing. Plus, I betcha they'll charge him with Alejandro's murder."

"Damn right they'll charge him. 5-0 sees a guy leaving the scene of a murder with a car full of drugs, and it's all over, nigga."

"I hope they rough him up something good." Sonny grinned. "Can you believe things worked out even better than we thought? Darkman's locked up, he's gonna get charged with some serious shit, and Crow and Leanne are too pussy to stick around. This means we don't have to give up no territory!"

"Word."

Sonny switched to a hip-hop station. We grooved to the music like two homies in their first ride. I put down the windows to spread the tunes to the public.

After dropping off the rental car, we went to Sonny's crib. Desarae was making French toast in her slinky Victoria's Secret bathrobe.

"Des, slap on a few pieces for me and Ty. We celebrating!"

"Sure thing, sweets. Take a look at the news. They might recap the car chase."

I looked at Sonny. "She knows?"

"Course she knows. She's my girl."

We sat in front of the TV and flicked channels, but couldn't find the car chase. In the meantime, we ate the delicious French toast.

I watched Desarae curl against Sonny's side.

Alyse.

I shoveled more food into my mouth. I had to forget about her.

At 12:30, a newsbreak on CBS-2 gave us an aerial clip of the car chase.

Sonny clapped his hands. "Look at that! He driving like a madman!"

"A wonder he didn't mow nobody down," Desarae said.

"Thank God for that," I muttered, and finished my French toast.

For the rest of the day, I walked around in a daze. It was a satisfied kind of daze that came from things going my way. Maybe now that Darkman was out of the picture, Alyse could come back into my life.

That night, as I sat in front of the computer, an e-mail from Alyse popped up in my inbox. My eyes bugged out.

When I opened the e-mail, I cursed. It was a damn message from Amnesty International asking me to sign an online petition to save some woman who was gonna be stoned to death in Africa. Alyse sent the e-mail to everybody she knew.

Instead of pressing delete, I pressed reply.

I wrote: *So I'm still on your list?*

Less than two minutes later, I got an answer. *Sorry about that. I'll delete your name.*

I wrote: *You don't have to. It was a very interesting message about that woman in Africa. I signed the petition.*

She wrote back: *That's B.S. Why are you always pretending to be someone you're not?*

My fingers shook over the keyboard as I tried to think of an answer.

In the end, I wrote: *My feelings for you are real.*

I waited for her answer, refreshing my screen every few seconds. I hoped she'd instant message me. That would be an easier way to have a conversation.

Five minutes passed, then ten. She didn't answer.

Fifteen minutes.

Damn it, she *had* to answer.

Caving in, I instant-messaged her: *Are you there?*

The message that came back was: *Your ID has been blocked by the user.*

I stared at the screen.

DOWN FOR THE COUNT

IN THE DAYS AFTER DARKMAN GOT ARRESTED, I WORKED harder than ever, wanting to prove to myself and anybody who didn't know it that I was still the King of the Streets.

I got myself an apartment, a seventh-floor, two-bedroom on Washington Avenue. The building wasn't much to look at on the outside, but my crib was a different story. I spiffed it up with a fly stereo system and a huge plasma-screen TV. I bought black leather furniture, had the hardwood floors shined up, and even got some African artwork for the walls. For the first time, the king had his own castle.

Mom didn't like it one bit. Her nerves were shot these days. I had a helluva time convincing her that I wasn't up to no good. Didn't have a prayer of convincing her that the shooting was a random drive-by.

I don't think she believed anything I said anymore. But there was nothing she could do, and she knew it.

For Mom and her family, Christmas Eve was a big deal, so I made sure I showed up. Every year they went back to the old neighborhood in Crown Heights, went to church, and had a feast at Aunt Mary and Uncle Phil's. I skipped church, but caught up with them at the party.

"Ty!" Mom threw herself into my arms. "I'm glad you're here."

"Course I am. It's Christmas!"

Aunt Sherise and Aunt Doris came up. It's a wonder they hugged me instead of knocking me upside the head. I guess Mom told them to be good.

We went into the living room. Everybody was there. They all looked at me with a lot more interest than usual. Whatever. I was expecting it.

I made the rounds, doing my best to answer questions about school (I'm going back soon), living by myself (I work at the gym, so that's how I can afford it), and my future goals (I want to be a personal trainer). It sucked that they all seemed to be extra careful around me, like they didn't want to say the wrong thing. But I guess that was better than having to answer questions about the drive-by.

Throughout the evening, I kept thinking about Alyse and wondering what she was doing. Was she at a family thing like me? Damn, she should be here, by my side.

It was a pipe dream.

Eventually I made it to the food table. There was fried chicken, ribs, catfish, pork chops, sweet potatoes, scallop potatoes, coleslaw, asparagus, cornbread. On Christmas, we always ate like crazy.

"Hello, Ty."

"G!" I gave my grandma a big hug. She was so short and light, I lifted her clear off the floor.

I started calling her G—for Grandma, not gangsta—years ago.

"You look great, G."

"Thanks." She craned her neck to look up at me. "Baby, I think you still growing."

"Sorry, G, but I think you're shrinking."

"You little—!"

Yeah, me and G always got along good.

"Your mama's so happy you're spending Christmas with her," she said, loading up her plate. "You gave us a scare, you know. Your poor mama's been worried sick."

"I'm all better now."

"That hasn't stopped her worrying. She's afraid you're turning out like Orlando."

I blinked. "C'mon, G, you know it ain't like that. Me and my dad are two different people."

"I hope so. Did she ever tell you why she left your father? She left him because of *you*."

"What did I have to do with it?"

"Your mama could've lived like a queen. But you were more important. She knew she couldn't raise you right if she was living with a hustler." G spooned some asparagus onto my plate. "You were brought up, Ty, not dragged up. And don't you forget it."

I spent the last few days of December working my ass off, going from one meeting place to another, delivering a few ki's here, a few there, and coming home late at night to a silence that even my fly stereo couldn't cover up.

The week before New Year's, Sonny and me met with Jones and Menendez to pick up a shipment. I didn't give them details on what went down with Darkman, but I let them know that we were the ones who brought him down. I could tell they were impressed.

But when we left the meeting, Sonny said, "It's about time we got ourselves new suppliers."

"Why? They holding up their end."

He stared at me. "You serious? What about them pictures? We supposed to forget that they threatened our peeps?"

"I told you, there wasn't nothing behind it. They were just sending a message. Look, I'll do some research. It could take a few weeks, and I ain't rushing into anything, but I'll try."

"Do that. I will too. We bound to find people."

In the next few days, I put feelers out for new suppliers, but all the leads I got were too shady to go after.

What Sonny didn't get was that in a business like ours, you weren't gonna be working with no Boy Scouts.

The question wasn't: Is this nigga dangerous?

It was: How dangerous is he?

THE SOUND OF THE LATE BELL

A FEW DAYS BEFORE NEW YEAR'S, I DECIDED TO CATCH UP WITH Monfrey.

When I stopped by the local bowling lanes where he hung out, he wasn't there. The homies said they hadn't seen him around for a week.

My instincts went off like a warning bell. Actually, it felt more like the late bell at school—once you heard it, you were already too late.

My next stop was the park where he liked to chill and smoke up.

No sign of him.

His favorite diner.

Still no sign.

Another nearby park.

Nothing.

I was running out of options. If I wasn't going to waste more time looking, I had to do something I didn't want to: go to his crib.

Rob Monfrey lived with his mom in a shit project where Flatbush and Crown Heights gangbangers shoot each other weekly. In front of the buildings were huge frozen piles of dirt, like the City tried to do something to fix up the neighborhood—but quit for the winter.

Stepping over a bum hunched up in the side doorway, I skipped stairs to the third floor. I couldn't remember his apartment number, but I was pretty sure it was the first door on the left.

I knocked.

"Monfrey, it's Ty!"

I banged on the door.

Nothing.

Cursing, I went back down the stairs.

The damn bum was now all laid out in the doorway, making it impossible for me to get by. I nudged him with my shoe. *"Yo, could you move?"*

The bum twitched like he just woke up. "Uhhh . . ." His groggy face looked up from under a nappy Afro.

"*Monfrey?*"

"Eh . . ."

I bent down. "Monfrey, it's me, Ty! You know me?"

"Tyyy . . ."

I went through his pockets until I found the crumpled lit-tle Ziploc bag. "*Damn*, Monfrey."

He slumped against the wall.

"What were you thinking? You told me you'd never touch that shit!"

He started shaking.

"Keys, where your keys?" I felt the rest of his pockets, but couldn't find them. Maybe that's why he ended up in the doorway instead of in his crib.

What the hell was I gonna do with him?

Leave him to rot.

Could I do that? Could I just leave him here?

Monfrey got himself fucked up. It wasn't my fault. He was supposed to stay away from anything stronger than weed.

But I couldn't leave him.

With the help of a cab driver (and an extra twenty bucks), I put Monfrey on my couch. The brother a mess. Shaking, sweating, puking. Begging for a hit. And when I wouldn't give it to him, he cursed me, my mama, and the day I was born. I was seeing a different person. A damn scary person. It was the crack talking, not Monfrey.

I couldn't take the look or the stink of him, but I knew if I left the apartment, he wouldn't stay put. He'd be on the streets trying to get the hit that would end the hell he was going through. I couldn't let that happen. I moved him into my bedroom so he couldn't sneak out without going past me. He tried to bounce twice that first night, but both times I stopped him. He didn't put up much of a fight, he was too weak. I dragged him back into the bedroom and shut the door. He started crying like a baby. And when he cried enough, he fell asleep.

The next day was just as bad. I thought I was gonna lose it. I couldn't get him to eat, sleep, or sit still. Finally I gave him a little weed to ease the pain. It helped. The shaking stopped.

"Where's your mom, Monfrey?"

"She in . . . Trinidad."

"When's she coming back?"

"I can't remember."

"I'm gonna put on a DVD for you now, and get you some food."

"Food. Yeah."

Damn, he was skin and bones. It was hard even looking at him.

"What you want to eat? I ain't got any food. We have to order something."

"There's a deli . . . on the corner. I'll go." He tried to get up.

"Sit down. I ain't letting you outta my sight."

"The fuck is this? House arrest?"

"Call it what you want. When I get your mom's okay, you're going up north."

Monfrey almost dropped his blunt. "Huh?"

"Not to jail, Monfrey. To rehab. I'm sending you somewhere cushy. Maybe you'll see some celebs."

"Fuck you, Ty. I done so much for you, and you wanna lock me up?"

"Fuck you, too, Monfrey. Now what you want to eat?"

HAPPY NEW YEAR

NEW YEAR'S DAY. I WOKE UP FEELING LIKE I DIDN'T SLEEP AT all. Pieces of a nightmare bugged me like a fly behind a curtain, but I didn't want to think about them.

I was in my own bed again, thank God. I finally got rid of Monfrey yesterday, when his mom came back from Trinidad. She looked like she was gonna whoop his ass, but I knew she'd take care of him. I told her about the arrangements I made for him to go into rehab. When I said I was paying for it, she didn't look surprised. I guess she knew that Monfrey worked for me. For all I knew, Monfrey could've told her himself.

My cell phone was blinking. Whenever my phone rang or I had a message, I couldn't help thinking it could be Alyse. I don't know why—there was no way that girl would change her mind about me.

I had three messages from last night.

"Ty, it's your boy, Cheddar. What's cracking? You over getting shot up? Me and the homies is partying at Brown's Billiards, so if you around, stop by."

Good thing I missed that one. I wasn't up for partying last night, not after the hellish few days with Monfrey. I'd locked myself in for the night, turned off my phone, looked at some porn mags, and stared at the ceiling until I fell asleep.

Message two was Sonny: *"Ty, it's around nine, why ain't you answering your phone? Just to let you know, I found us some new suppliers, and we got a nice little shipment coming in. I figure we'll put the shit out, see how the peeps like it. We'll meet the shipment down at Brighton Beach at one thirty the day after tomorrow. Later."*

When I heard the voice on the third message, I couldn't believe it. *"Hi, it's Alyse. I know it's been a while."* I could hear the catch in her voice. *"I'm just calling, well, to wish you a Happy New Year and . . . and to apologize for how bitchy I was over the e-mail that time. School isn't the same without you. I told our teachers you weren't coming back, and they were really disappointed. They still ask about you. Anyway, you don't need to call back, I just wanted you to know . . . that I hope you're okay. Happy New Year."*

I listened to her message again. Did she miss me? I listened to it a third time. It came at 11:30 last night. Did that mean she was thinking about me at midnight?

When she said "you don't need to call back," did that mean *don't call back* or *you don't have to call back, but I want you to?*

Women! No, not women. One woman: Alyse. I lay back on my bed, thinking about how it felt to hold her in my arms.

Damn. Why she gotta be so stubborn? Why couldn't she accept the real me?

Or was I wrong about that? Maybe she wanted to accept who I was, just not what I did for a living. Maybe they weren't the same thing.

If she called me, did that mean she might take me back? All I had to do was quit the business.

All I had to do was quit the business.

It was the first time I thought of it. I could quit.

But who would I be if I walked away?

So much went through my brain, it felt like my head was gonna burst. *How would I leave the business how would I make money how would Dad react what would Sonny do without me what would I do with my life? You can't get out it's not realistic you the King of the Streets you have a vision a vision of where you'll be and what you'll be—a hustler who makes mad dough and never ever gets caught . . .*

Thoughts of all kinds came at me, like a crocodile spinning in a death roll. I just let it happen.

CHOICES

THE NEXT DAY I WENT THROUGH THE METAL DETECTORS AT
Les Chancellor.

"Johnson, you look good. How you feeling?"

"Real good, Rosie. I'm coming back to school."

"Yeah? Thought we'd seen the last of you." She looked across the machine to the other guard. "Pete, you hear that? He's back."

"Good for you, Johnson."

"Thanks." I walked toward the main office to speak to Ms. Gottlieb, the principal. I'd never talked to her before, but I'd seen her around. The lady was always in the halls, ready to scream at anybody who wasn't where they were supposed to be.

In the office, I went up to the main desk. "Excuse me, ma'am?"

A middle-aged secretary with poofy black hair looked up from her computer. "Yes?"

"I'm here to see Ms. Gottlieb. Could you tell her Ty Johnson's here?"

Her head snapped sideways. I knew right away that she was the secretary I dicked around on the phone a few months ago. "Have you scheduled an appointment, *Mis-ter* Johnson?"

"No, but it's real important."

"I should hope it's important if it's the principal you're wanting to see. Unfortunately, this is a very busy time of year for her. I can book you an appointment for next week."

"Next week? Are you kidding?"

Her face wasn't kidding. "Should I book it or not?"

I took a breath. Could I wait until next week?

No, I couldn't.

"Don't book it. This can't wait."

"I can't imagine what it is that can't wait until next week. You are no longer attending this school. Did you forget something?"

"Look, I only need a few minutes of her time. I'll wait, it don't matter how long it takes. Please just tell her I'm here."

"I'll tell her. But I'm not making any promises."

"That's fine. Thanks for your help."

I took a seat and waited. I wasn't gonna budge.

An hour went by. I wouldn't let myself check my phone messages. It would just be Sonny cursing me out for missing the exchange, and I didn't want to deal with that right now.

More time went by. A few kids came to sign out early, always with notes from parents, doctors, or parole officers.

And then Alyse walked in. Without seeing me, she signed the attendance book. "I'm taking my son to a doctor's appointment," she told the secretary. "I don't have an appointment slip with me, but I'll bring one tomorrow."

On her way out, Alyse saw me. Her eyes widened. "Ty!"

My tongue froze. All I could do was nod.

"What are you doing here? Are you seeing Ms. Gottlieb?"

"Yeah."

"You're coming back to school?"

"I hope so."

"Great! I'm really glad for you. Anyway, I better go — I'm taking Gavin to the doctor. See ya."

She hurried out.

Over the next hour, I saw the principal twice, once leaving her office, and then returning a few minutes later. She didn't even look my way. I started to wonder if the secretary ever told her I was there.

Then the principal's door opened, and finally, *finally*, she looked my way. "Tyrone Johnson. Come in quickly."

I didn't need no encouragement.

"Sit. Now tell me what this is about."

I cleared my throat. "I wanna come back to Les Chancellor."

She looked at a piece of paper on her desk. The paper was part of a file. My file.

"I know of your hospital stay. The school was unable to contact you after you were released. You were no longer living with your mother." She looked at me over her glasses. "Is this accurate?"

"Yes, ma'am. I know I should've come back sooner, but I was really busy. I had to do lots of physical therapy."

"It was your responsibility to inform the school of your status, Mr. Johnson. On what grounds do you want us to consider your reapplication?"

"Well, as you said, I had serious medical stuff. Plus, I never got kicked out or nothing, so I figure . . . on those grounds."

"Truancy for more than three days without justification is the equivalent of expulsion. I'm sure that was explained to you when you first came here. I will ask you again, why should we let you back in?" As I was opening my mouth, she reminded me, "The truth, please."

"After I got shot, I admit, school was the last thing on my mind. I never been a big fan of school, but here, things were okay for me. I learned a few things, met some good people. Most of my teachers were cool. Coming here gives me a reason to get up in the morning."

She took off her glasses. "Most of the students who ask for readmission have an ulterior motive. It's usually that they have a court date coming up and want to impress the judge by saying they're in school." Before I could say anything, she went on, "But I do not believe that is the case with you."

I relaxed a little.

"I'll send memos to your teachers asking for their recommendations. If they feel you would benefit by readmission, I will place you on our roster for the fall."

"Huh? It's only January. The second semester's about to start."

"That isn't the issue. There is currently a waiting list to get into this school. At present, the list has eighty-four students. Your position has already been filled."

I was speechless.

"I will do my best to ensure that you will be with us in the fall. I can do no more than that. I recommend that you find another school that will take you. If you like, you can schedule an appointment with a guidance counselor who will help you find a space in another school."

I felt like sinking through the floor. Going back to Les Chancellor was the one thing, the only thing, I was set on. How could I wait until September to come back?

"I'm sorry, Tyrone. Don't get discouraged. You stay on the right track, and we'll be pleased to have you in the fall."

"Thanks, Ms. Gottlieb." Like a zombie, I got up. I walked out of the office and through the empty hallway.

Outside, it was getting dark. It was cold, and the breeze was picking up.

I stood at the bus stop, not caring when it came. I wasn't even sure it was the wind that made my eyes water.

Taking my cell phone from my pocket, I saw six messages.

'Course, one after the other was from Sonny, asking where the hell I was at.

The next message was from Desarae. She was hysterical. I couldn't make out what she saying.

The last one was from Gary, Sonny's neighbor. He was choked up. *"Ty . . . God, some bad shit went down. They found Sonny at Brighton Beach, all shot up. He didn't have a chance."*

TAKEN

BY THE TIME I GOT TO SONNY'S, POLICE WERE EVERYWHERE.
Gary was barefoot in the hallway.

"Ty!" He gave me a rough, one-arm hug. "Where you been?"

I followed him back into his apartment, closing the door after us.

My voice was far away, like it came from outside me. "Where's Desarae? She in there with the cops?"

"Her sister came and got her. When the cops told her Sonny got killed, she flipped out. She just kept screaming and screaming. . . ."

"What happened?"

"The cops ain't saying nothing about the circumstances— just that they found him at Brighton Beach." He took hold of my arm, like he thought my legs were gonna buckle. "I'm so sorry, man. Y'always been Sonny's dog."

I stepped back and leaned against the wall. Sonny was dead. *Sonny.* I was living one of my nightmares.

"Ty, you better sit down. Let me get you a beer or something."

"No thanks, Gary. I have to talk to the police."

Gary did a double take. "You ain't serious. What you gonna say?"

"I don't know yet."

"Then stay out of it, son. Trust me. Pigs ain't nothing but trouble."

"They'll come knocking, anyway. Better I go to them. I got nothing to hide."

"*Ty*, you tripping! You want the cops to know that you a hustla?"

"They already know."

"So? You wanna give them reason to ride your ass from now on? You wanna live like that?"

I didn't have an answer to that. I went toward the door.

Gary said, "Man, whatever went down at Brighton Beach, thank God you wasn't there."

"Maybe if I had Sonny's back, he'd still be alive."

• • •

The next few hours went by in a blur. I went to the local precinct, told them I was a friend of Sonny's and wanted to talk to someone.

They took me into an interview room. One of the officers put a cup of coffee into my hand. It tasted like mud, but I drank it.

Akindele came in. He didn't look surprised to see me. I bet nothing surprised him anymore.

"Thanks for coming in, Mr. Johnson. We appreciate your voluntary cooperation."

"I want to help any way I can. Did you talk to Sonny's girlfriend yet?"

"No. She's very distraught. Her sister asked us to conduct the interview tomorrow morning. Now, could you tell me the nature of your relationship to Sonny?"

"We friends. He been a friend of the family for years."

"Was he, specifically, a friend of your father's?"

"Yeah."

"What do you know about what happened today?"

"Sonny was supposed to make an exchange with a couple of guys. He never told me their names."

"What sort of exchange are you referring to?"

"Drugs for cash."

"What kind of drugs?"

"I don't know." It was true. Since I wasn't taking Sonny's calls for the past few days, I didn't have the 4-1-1 on the shipment.

"Will you guess?"

"Coke. Maybe heroin."

"Did your friend tell you how much money he was taking with him?"

"No, but he said the deal was pretty big. The money . . . it was probably in a blue nylon Nike bag. Sonny had a whole stash of them."

"As far as I know, we didn't see a stash of blue Nike bags at his apartment."

"Well, he probably keeps them someplace else."

Akindele nodded. "What do you think went wrong?"

"Sonny got scammed. They must've planned to kill him the whole time." I ran a hand over my scalp, trying to stay calm. I couldn't lose it now. This interview was too important.

"Did he say anything at all about the guys he was going to meet? What they looked like, where they came from, where he met them. . . ."

I shook my head. "We hadn't talked for a few days. I only

knew about the deal because he left me phone messages."

Akindele flipped back in his notepad. "His cell phone records show that he called you nine times in the past few days."

"Yeah, but I never answered the phone."

"Why not? You and Sonny on the outs?"

"No. I had other things on my mind."

"Like what?"

"I decided to go back to school. I tried to, anyway."

Akindele raised his eyebrows, but left it alone. He wrote some notes while I sat there staring at the lines in his wide forehead. Grief ate away at my insides.

I asked, "You got a plan to find Sonny's killers? I mean, I hope this is a real murder investigation, even though Sonny was a hustler."

"Don't worry, Mr. Johnson. It will receive the same attention as any other murder investigation." He opened the folder on the table and took out two pictures. "Do you recognize these men?"

I looked at the pictures, but had to shake my head. "Why? They got something to do with Sonny's murder?"

"That's what I intend to find out. There was a similar incident in the Bronx a few months ago. The victim was shot, but he survived and was able to identify the shooters. Their names are William Mathieu and Devin Harrison. We're trying to track them down. Do you have any idea where Sonny might have first come into contact with the men who killed him?"

"No."

"You must know some of Sonny's hangouts." He flipped his notepad to a new page and gave me a pen. "I'd like you to write them down for me."

I stopped. The guys at those places didn't talk to cops.

"You want us to solve your friend's murder, don't you?"

"Yeah." I wrote down a couple of places, figuring my best bet was to get there before the cops did and ask questions myself.

I slid the pad back to him. "Can I get copies of these?" I picked up the pictures. "In case I run into somebody who knows them?"

Akindele's eyes narrowed, but he nodded. "I'll get copies for you."

Over the next few minutes he kept questioning me, but I couldn't give him any good information. Finally he said, "You've been helpful, Mr. Johnson. If you think of anything else, please call me." He gave me his card.

"Thanks." I knew that I hadn't been helpful, not really. I

just didn't know enough to help the investigation.

But that was about to change.

Desarae's sister, Maydean, lived in a housing project on Avenue X, across from Sheepshead Bay High School. I was at her place for parties a few times. I buzzed her apartment.

"Hello?"

"Maydean, it's Ty Johnson. Can I come up?"

She buzzed me in.

I stepped into the elevator, staring at the floor the whole way up. I tried not to think or feel, but instead focus on what I had to do.

When Maydean opened the door and I saw Desarae sitting on the couch, I almost lost it. She looked up at me through dead eyes. I went to her, wrapped my arms around her. I felt her nails digging into my shirt.

I held her for a while. Nobody spoke.

She broke away to blow her nose. There was a distance in her eyes, a blank something that told me she was on tranquilizers. I didn't blame her.

I said, "I gotta ask you a few questions so that we can catch the guys who did this."

She nodded.

• • •

Around ten o'clock that night I went into a bar so shady that it didn't have a sign outside with a name. If it wasn't for Desarae, I wouldn't even know this place was here.

The place had the stink of stale beer, old vomit, and cigarettes. It was almost empty, with a few loners sitting at little round tables. I went up to the bar and sat down two stools away from a drunk guy who was talking to himself.

The bartender—dark hair, maybe thirty-five, needed a shave—came up to me. "How are ya?"

"A'ight. You?"

"Surviving. What can I getcha?"

"Corona."

"Lime?"

"No thanks."

He gave me the drink, and I paid him up front. "Hey, have you seen Sonny Blake tonight?" I asked.

"If he said he'll be here, he'll be here." He used a rag to wipe some drops off the bar. "That guy doesn't disappoint."

"I ain't really meeting Sonny tonight. I just wanted to make sure you knew him before I told you what happened. What's your name?"

"James."

"James, Sonny was shot today—by guys he met in this bar last Thursday night."

He blinked. "*What?*"

"He's dead."

"Holy shit."

"You remember seeing Sonny with two guys last Thursday?"

James wouldn't look at me. He kept wiping the bar.

"Did you set up the meeting between Sonny and those guys?"

His head shot up. "I don't get involved in what goes on here."

"Right. But do you know what I'm talking about?"

"You sound like a cop."

I laughed. "No way. Hell, I ain't even old enough to be in here." I showed him my driver's licence.

"That could be fake." He looked closer. "Wait . . . Ty Johnson?"

"Heard of me?"

"Sonny talked about you. Said you're Orlando Johnson's son. You're business partners."

That was Sonny. He trusted people too much.

"I'll be straight with you, James. I only care about one

thing: Sonny's killers going down. I need your help." I put the pictures in front of him. "These the guys?"

He nodded. "I never saw them before three weeks ago. Then they started coming in every other night. They kept to themselves. One of them had a strong accent, Haitian, maybe."

"You hear what they talked about with Sonny?"

"No. I figured they were making a deal of some kind. Do the cops know what happened?"

"All they know is that Sonny was found at Brighton Beach with three bullets in him. I told them why he was there."

"You told them Sonny was a dealer?"

"They already knew that. I didn't have much more to tell them."

"Well, can my ID of these fellas help?"

"It can help a lot. If you don't want the cops questioning you here, go to the precinct and give your statement. Ask for Detective Akindele."

"I'll go over in the morning."

"Thanks, man."

When I walked out of the bar, the cold January wind slapped my face.

Sonny was really gone.

BLACK JANUARY

WHEN I GOT OUT OF BED AT 12:30 THE NEXT DAY, IT was just because my body wouldn't sleep no more.

The crib was cold. Damn landlord turned the heat down because he thought people were working during the day. Not *this* tenant. I'd call him later and give him hell.

I stared at my blinking phone like it was covered with bugs. I didn't want to touch it. But I had to.

The message was from Desarae. She told me that she was meeting Sonny's mom and sister at the Jamieson Funeral Home on Flatbush at four o'clock. She hoped to see me there.

Funeral arrangements for Sonny? My stomach felt sick.

There was other messages from homies asking about Sonny. I paid them no mind.

No message from Alyse. I don't know why I even thought there might be.

I went to the kitchen. In the fridge, I had a half-carton of milk, but the only cereal box around was sticking out of the garbage. I didn't have nothing in the cupboards but a box of crackers, instant coffee, and sugar. No way I was touching those crackers, not when Monfrey's hand was in there.

I made the coffee and sat down in front of the TV. I surfed from channel to channel, finally choosing a sports station. Sonny kept popping up in my mind. I turned up the sound to get my mind somewhere else.

Out of nowhere, my stomach heaved. I ran to the bathroom and threw up. When it was over, I hugged the toilet, worn out, resting my head on the toilet seat.

I sniffed. Tears squeezed out from under my eyelids. They kept coming. Memories of Sonny kept coming.

He was gone, that crazy-ass nigga who was the closest thing to a brother I ever had.

He was gone.

And it might've been my fault.

If I hadn't been so wrapped up in my own problems, I could've convinced him not to risk the deal.

If I hadn't let him down, Sonny could still be living and breathing right now.

And I had to live with that for the rest of my life.

HONORING THE DEAD

THE DAY OF THE FUNERAL WAS BLUE-SKIED AND FREEZING cold. I walked to the church, thinking the air would do me good. Instead, I got there with frozen hands, ears, and feet.

Inside the church, organ music played. The room was more than half full. Not a bad crowd, but Sonny would've wanted more.

I walked up a side aisle. I saw a bunch of homies from the hood, including Sonny's neighbor, Gary. Most of them had on suit jackets, some even had on ties, and their hats and do-rags were off out of props for Sonny. A few of our long-term customers were there too.

I squeezed into the first row beside a woman who said she was Fayola, Sonny's aunt. His sister, his mom, and Desarae all said hi to me.

The organ music stopped, and the minister walked in. He was a big-shouldered man about sixty, in a black robe and a red stole. When he reached the pulpit and started to speak, his voice was deep but soft.

I hadn't gone to church in years. When I was little, I actually wanted to go to church, mostly because of the great music. But as I got older and started to understand what the minister was saying, I didn't like it anymore. Too much of the minister's talk was about the temptation of the streets and the evil of drugs. I didn't feel comfortable in a place where they told me my dad was a sinner.

Sonny's aunt read the scripture. Then it was my turn to talk. Taking a deep breath, I walked up to the pulpit.

"Sonny was one of a kind. He was the closest thing I ever had to a brother." My throat tightened around my words.

Get it together. Ty Johnson don't lose control.

I cleared my throat and raised my head. "Sonny was the type of guy who liked to be noticed, huh?"

People nodded and chuckled. One shouted, "Amen!"

"One of his favorite things to do was go to fancy restaurants decked out one hundred percent gangsta, just to see the look on people's faces. Sonny didn't care what people thought of him, because he knew who he was. He knew what was important to him, and that was people. The people here today. He was always taking care of his mom and his sister. He was so into his girl Desarae that he wanted to get the words 'Desarae, My Queen' tattooed on his arm. He would've done it too."

I glanced at Desarae, who tried to smile.

"To me, Sonny was a great friend. He was the type of guy you could call at three in the morning with a problem and he wouldn't complain. And he wasn't shy to give a homey a hug if he needed it. I ain't saying I ever needed it." People laughed.

"Some of you know that a few weeks ago, I was in the hospital. For a couple days, it was pretty serious. They wouldn't let nobody in but family. Well, Sonny wouldn't have it." I looked up to see people nodding, smiling. "The hospital staff knew I didn't have a brother, but Sonny was tripping so much that they let him see me, just to keep the peace."

I waited until the laughter died down before going on. "I don't know if anybody can picture a world without Sonny. I know I can't. Maybe we don't have to. Maybe if we keep remembering him, all the good times we had with him, he'll still be with us. I know that's what he'd want. Sonny, we'll never forget you. Peace."

A WALK IN THE PARK

THAT NIGHT I TOOK A WALK IN PROSPECT PARK, CARRYING Sonny's loss on me like a lead backpack.

I walked because my crib felt like a prison closing in on me. I walked because I had nowhere to go.

I didn't wanna face the truth.

Nobody lasts in this business. Not for long, anyway. Not Dad. Not Sonny. Even Jimmy Pennington couldn't last at the top.

Why the hell couldn't I admit that until now?

The reason was at Sing Sing, probably lifting weights and talking trash with his buddies. He always used me, and I always knew it. But I let it happen. It wasn't just because I made stacks of cash. It was because I felt sorry for him, being locked up and all. He always told me that knowing I was running the business was what kept him going.

Fuck it.

Day by day, year by year, the business took away anything good in my life. Alyse, Mom, Monfrey, Sonny—everybody I cared about was getting hurt or killed.

Hell, I didn't even have *school* no more. At least there, I felt normal. As wack as school sometimes was, I kind of missed the debates in Mr. Guzman's class or chilling with my homies in the cafeteria.

Fact was, I didn't even know who Ty Johnson was anymore.

I sucked in cold air. I thought that after bringing Darkman down, I'd be on top, the King of the Streets. But I was wrong.

You are becoming your father.

There it was again, those thoughts in my head so intense, they were like voices.

You are becoming your father.

But if I was becoming my dad, why did I have a guilty conscience? One of Orlando's strengths was that he did whatever had to be done without hesitation or emotion.

Did that make him strong, or did that make him a fucking psycho?

DEAR DAD

THE NEXT MORNING I GOT A CALL FROM A PRISON VOLUNTEER that my dad wanted to see me.

I knew it was coming.

Orlando was always keeping tabs. He would've known the funeral was yesterday, and he'd want to talk about what Sonny's death meant for the business.

There was no point in putting off the visit. When Orlando called, I came.

I walked up to the gates of Sing Sing. I felt the cold concrete and slippery black ice under my feet. The sky was dark gray. I knew there wouldn't be sunlight today.

In the visitors' room, Dad gave me a strong pat on the back and a shoulder squeeze. "Son."

We sat down.

"What the hell happened, Ty? How'd you two end up dealing with those thugs?"

"Sonny was looking to get some new suppliers. I guess he thought we could get a better deal than we was getting with Jones and Menendez." I wasn't gonna tell him about their threats. The last thing I needed was more trouble.

"Wait a minute, what do you mean, *you guess* he was looking for a better deal? You weren't in on the decision?"

"No."

His hands tightened in front of him. "You better explain."

"It was Sonny's deal, not mine. I didn't want to get new suppliers. I couldn't stop him."

"But you in charge, Ty! You just let Sonny do what he wanted?" He slammed his fist on the table. "You kidding me?"

A guard nearby said, "*Easy, Johnson.*"

"I'm cool," Orlando said. Then he looked at me. "I don't get it. We talked about this. Sonny wasn't the sharpest knife in the drawer. You was supposed to keep an eye on him."

"I wish . . . I wish I had. Like I said, I was busy with other things. Sonny made the call. A real bad call."

"Damn right, it was a bad one. He's in a fucking box! And you would be, too, if you was there."

"Yeah, well, I wasn't there."

"Real convenient for you, boy. See what happens when you *don't* get involved, *don't* use your God-given brains? People go down. Do you realize how hard it is to replace someone like Sonny? How many years of trust and loyalty we built up? You think we can bring in any nigga off the street and trust him like we trusted Sonny?"

"Sonny's dead, Dad. That's more important than losing an employee."

"I ain't buying this sentimental crap from you, Ty. I'm as broken up as you that Sonny went down, but it don't change the fact that you fucked up."

"Look, Dad, I'm gonna have to live with Sonny's death for the rest of my life, so don't throw that shit at me."

"Well, from now on, you don't have to worry about Sonny's back. Just yours." He put his hand over mine. "The business is totally on your shoulders now."

"I don't want it, Dad. I want out."

Only when I said the words did I realize that I'd finally made up my mind.

"What you say?"

"The business. Everything. I'm out."

"You playing."

"I'm dead serious."

"Don't fuck with me, Ty."

"I ain't. Nothing you can say will change my mind, so don't even try."

"How could you even *think* of walking away from all I built?"

"*I* built it, too, Dad. I kept it going for five years. But now I'm finished with it."

His hand tightened on mine. "Tell me where you got this idea of quitting the business. You scared you'll end up like Sonny?"

"It ain't about being scared. It's about being smart. And yeah, I don't wanna end up dead. Or locked up."

My hand was trapped under his. If he squeezed tighter, he'd snap a bone.

"Y-You have to find somebody else to take over the business, D-Dad. I-I ain't making one more deal."

"But you the only one I can trust!"

"I'm s-sorry, Dad."

Purple veins bulged in his head. "I ain't coming outta this hellhole to find I got no business!" He let go of my hand, throwing it away like I had a disease.

"When you get out, you can get the old customers back,

or get new ones. You still got the account. There's almost two hundred Gs."

"That's jack shit compared to what my business is worth!"

"Dad, I'm sorry if you think I let you down."

He wouldn't even look at me. "Those are just words, Ty. That ain't gonna give me my life back when I get outta here."

The fight was out of his voice. Now he just sounded broken.

UNDER CONSTRUCTION

"JOHNSON, BUDDY, HOW ARE YA?"

The phone woke me up. I squinted at my alarm clock: 1:37 a.m. "Jimmy?"

"Yep. You haven't returned my calls. And I've got customers waiting."

"I told you I ain't hustling no more."

"Look, I don't blame you for not wanting to do business with me after I freaked out on you that time. Gimme another chance, will ya? I was all fucked up because my girlfriend left me. I'm back on my feet now. I've got twenty grand burning a hole in my pocket and a bunch of clients depending on me."

"You ain't listening to me, Jimmy. I said *I'm outta the business.*"

"Ty Johnson walking away from the game? I don't believe it."

"That's up to you. I'm going back to sleep."

"Wait! Tell me what's going on, Ty. Something got you spooked?"

"Let's just say I figured out this business is a dead end."

He was quiet for a few seconds. "So will you hook me up with another supplier?"

That was Jimmy. Always a businessman. Still a junkie.

"Don't take it personal, Jimmy. But I think you should give your clients their money back and check yourself into rehab."

"*What?* Don't turn this around on me, Johnson. You're the one who can't keep up. I'll find another supplier, then."

"Do what you gotta do." I hung up.

REVISITING MONFREY

A FEW WEEKS LATER, I WALKED INTO THAI TAKE-OUT AND looked up at the menu. "I'll take a number six."

"Me too." I turned around to see Rob Monfrey. He looked heavier and healthier than I'd ever seen him. We slapped hands.

We got our food and sat down. I said, "Thanks for meeting me, man. It's been a while. How you feeling?"

"Clean." He tapped a finger against his temple. "And clear, son. Clearer than I ever was. I ain't saying it don't still hurt sometimes. What about you? I heard some of your old customers be giving you a hard time."

"That ain't news. Still the eyes and ears of Brooklyn, huh?"

"That'll never change. There be a lot of niggas wanting to take your place, you know."

"I know. A couple of 'em even tried to get me to hook them up with my suppliers. I told them where to go. I ain't taking sides."

"You think there'll be trouble?"

"Maybe. I don't see one of the new hustlers rising to the top yet. If it don't happen soon, there'll be blood. But that ain't my problem."

"I heard they caught Sonny's killers."

"Yeah. Trial is next year."

Monfrey must've heard the rumors. Rumors that I was freaked out by Sonny's death. Rumors that I made money off it.

I didn't care what anybody thought, since I had my own guilt to deal with.

It kept me plenty busy.

I changed the topic. "So you back at Sheepshead now?"

"Nah. They put me at your old school, Les Chancellor."

I almost dropped my fork. "You at Les Chancellor?"

"Uh-huh. Edelstone pulled some strings."

"You lucky."

"I am?"

"Yeah. They wouldn't let me back in when I asked. Hey, there's this girl I used to know. . . ."

"Alyse." He scooped in more food. It took him a year to chew and swallow. "Yeah, I know her. When she found out I was from Sheepshead, she asked if I knew you. I said, *You bet your ass I know him!*"

"What she say about me?"

"She said you used to be good friends. She missed having you around school."

"Is that all she said?"

He scratched his head. "Well, something like that."

"Think, Monfrey. What *exactly* did she say?"

He slurped his drink. "What I told you. That's what she said."

"What was the look on her face?"

Monfrey put on a sad, lovesick face.

"You playing?"

"Exaggerating, maybe. But that girl got a thing for you. And you got a thing for her. What happened?"

"She found out I was a hustler."

"So? Don't she know you quit the business?"

"No. We haven't talked in a while. But, anyway, quitting the business ain't enough. I lied to her. She'll never forgive me for that."

"C'mon man, don't you watch *Oprah*? Women love to

forgive. Show her a few tears and she'll be all yours."

"I don't know, Monfrey. That don't sound like me. Just do me a favor, will ya? If Alyse says something about me again, tell me."

"Sure." He grinned. "Kinda like old times, eh? Passing on information?"

"Right, but this time, I'll pay you in Thai food."

Monfrey laughed. "Deal."

ADULTS ONLY

ON THE MORNING OF FEBRUARY TWENTIETH, I WALKED INTO the office of a guidance counselor.

Ms. Anderson, a light-skinned lady with a weave in her hair and two cups of coffee on her desk, shook my hand. "Remind me of your name?"

"Tyrone Johnson."

"Right, you called. Please have a seat."

"Thanks."

"So, what brings you to the Adult High School?"

"Today's my eighteenth birthday, so I'm eligible."

"Oh, well Happy Birthday!" She looked at her desk calendar. "The second semester's been underway for almost three weeks. You'll have to work hard to catch up."

"I'll work hard."

She pulled her glasses from the top of her head to her

and I ain't on probation. All I'm asking for is a fresh start."

"That's what I wanted to hear." She smiled. "Welcome to the Adult High School."

I ended up taking eight courses. My schedule was every day from 8:30 a.m. to 1:20 p.m., and Monday and Thursday nights from 6 to 8:30 p.m. Flunking wasn't an option. I needed to do better than just pass if these credits were gonna help me.

An hour later I went to my first class. The bell just rang, so I walked in with a bunch of people. I'd thought people in the class would be twice my age, but they were mostly in their twenties.

I went up to the teacher, who was erasing the board from the last class.

"Are you Mr. Sallahi?" I asked.

"If not, I'm in the wrong place."

"I'm Ty Johnson. I'm starting here today."

"Nice to meet you, Ty. Have a seat and let's get started. You'll have a little catching up to do, but I'll discuss that with you later."

"Thanks."

I found an empty seat.

The second bell rang. As the class started, I looked around. Nobody knew who I was, or where I been.

I felt a smile come to my face. Here, in this classroom, I could be whoever I wanted to be.

nose. "Now let me take a look at your file. . . . Your old school sent it over. I thought we'd look at it together."

I swallowed, watching her flip through the stack of files on her desk.

"Maybe it's lost?"

She looked up and smiled, but kept going through the files. "If it is we'll just continue with the interview and— look! Here it is."

"It ain't that great."

Opening my file, I saw her eyes widen. "Coming from Les Chancellor, I see."

"Yes, ma'am."

"Your first two report cards look good, but in the third marking period you just seem to drop off the attendance roster. What happened?"

"I was in the hospital. After that, I lost my motivation to go back to school."

"Why were you in the hospital?"

I didn't like where this was going. "I got shot."

"I see. A gangbanger, are we?"

"No."

She flipped back through my file. "Well, it looks like you haven't been very serious about school over the years."

"School wasn't my thing. But I don't have a criminal record,

BIRTHDAY WISHES

I NEVER MADE A BIG DEAL ABOUT BIRTHDAYS. BUT I KNEW THIS birthday would be different from all the others.

Mom made me dinner last night. She figured I'd be going out with friends on my birthday, and I didn't correct her. Truth was, it was always Sonny that took me out and got me wasted.

I could've called up Cheddar or Monfrey and dropped some hints about my birthday, but I didn't. With Sonny gone, I didn't feel like celebrating.

Dad didn't call. It was no surprise.

After finishing my homework, I called up to order a pizza, then sat down and watched some TV.

I had more than a hundred channels and still couldn't find nothing interesting. Screw it. I popped in the *Terminator 2* DVD. Couldn't go wrong with that.

A while later, I heard the buzzer. I pressed the button to let the pizza man in and got the cash ready.

When the knock came, I swung open the door and stopped dead.

"Did I scare you?" Alyse grinned.

"Uh, no." I couldn't take my eyes off her.

"Can I come in?"

"Yeah, sorry." I backed into my crib. "Uh, let me get your coat."

"Thanks."

I put her coat in the hall closet. Was Alyse really here?

She kissed my cheek.

"What's that for?"

"It's a Happy Birthday kiss."

"How'd you know?"

"Don't you remember writing it in my student planner a few months ago? You took up the whole page."

I laughed, remembering.

We went into the living room.

"I hope I wasn't interrupting anything. Were you about to go out?"

"Nah." I sat down in the easy chair, and she sat too. "I was just chilling."

"I thought you might be heading out to a club."

"Since I hung out with you, I got to like staying in."

She smiled. "Well, maybe you have school tomorrow. Rob Monfrey told me you were going to register at the Adult High School today. How'd it go?"

"Good. I'm taking six courses in the daytime. Plus, I'll be going two nights a week."

"Wow."

"So Monfrey's been talking about me?"

"Yeah. That guy thinks a lot of you. He said he used to do errands for you. But he also told me that when he got hooked on crack, you took him in and forced him to get clean." Her eyes were soft. "He's thankful for that."

I didn't know what to say.

"I know you had a rough time the past few months. I heard about your friend Sonny."

I still wasn't sure what to say. I didn't deserve her sympathy.

"Rob said you quit the business."

"Yeah. I won't even sell you an Advil."

She laughed, but her face stayed serious. "Were you going to tell me? I mean, that you quit the business and decided to go back to school?"

"I was gonna send you a letter in June telling you everything."

She looked confused. "Why in June?"

"Because I wanted to give you a copy of my report card." I looked her straight in the eyes. "I wanted you to see me get all A's."

"Are you serious?"

"Dead serious. I wanted you to see the proof that I got it together."

"I already see the proof." She reached over to take my hand.

I squeezed hers back.

"I got you a birthday gift." She pulled a card out of her pocketbook and gave it to me.

I opened it. Two Knicks tickets dropped out.

"These are some hot seats, yo!"

She grinned.

"Alyse, wait. These tickets must've been mad expensive. Let's make a deal. I pay for the tickets and a babysitter, and you be nice enough to come to the game with me."

"Thanks for the offer, but the tickets didn't cost me anything."

"How's that?"

"I didn't want to go to that other Knicks game without you, so I scalped the tickets, thinking I'd buy us tickets in the future. I actually made a profit."

"Scalping tickets is illegal," I said, trying not to laugh.

"Well, I'm not going to make a business out of it."

"Good call."

Feeling bold, I moved over to the sofa. I had to be closer, to be surrounded by her. "Does this mean you're giving me a second chance?"

She nodded.

"Why?"

"Because you shine, Ty. Don't you know you shine?"

"I know I don't deserve you, Alyse." I took her face in my hands, and made her a promise. "But I will."

ALLISON VAN DIEPEN is a high school social studies teacher who is often mistaken for a student. She spent three and a half years teaching at one of Brooklyn's most dangerous public high schools. She now lives in Ottawa, Canada. This is her first novel.